DOWN WITH LOVE

"Look at all the stars!" Darlene tilted her head back to look up in awe. The entire night sky was glittering with brilliant stars and she had the feeling they were shining especially for her and Aaron.

"They are pretty, aren't they?" he agreed. They stopped at the passenger side of his car, but instead of opening the door, Aaron drew her into his arms. "I've been wanting to do this all night," he said huskily, and then he kissed her.

It wasn't like the first time they'd kissed, over almost before Darlene knew what was happening. This time his mouth lingered on hers, his lips warm, stealing the very breath out of her body. And Darlene knew absolutely, positively that she was head over heels in love with Aaron Caldwell.

Bantam titles in the Sweet Dreams series. Ask your bookseller for any of the following titles you have missed:

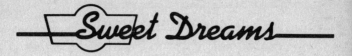

DOWN WITH LOVE

Carla Bracale

BANTAM BOOKS
NEW YORK · TORONTO · LONDON · SYDNEY · AUCKLAND

DOWN WITH LOVE!
A BANTAM BOOK 0 553 29144 0

First publication in Great Britain

PRINTING HISTORY
Bantam edition published 1992
Bantam edition reprinted 1995

Cover photo by Pat Hill

Bantam Books are published by Transworld Publishers Ltd,
61–63 Uxbridge Road, Ealing, London W5 5SA,
in Australia by Transworld Publishers (Australia) Pty Ltd,
15–25 Helles Avenue, Moorebank, NSW 2170,
and in New Zealand by Transworld Publishers (NZ) Ltd,
3 William Pickering Drive, Albany, Auckland.

Printed and bound in Great Britain by
Cox & Wyman Ltd, Reading, Berkshire.

DOWN WITH LOVE

Chapter One

Darlene Sullivan's hands trembled as she maneuvered her car into the narrow parking space. She turned off the engine and looked up at the entrance gates before her.

"Welcome to the Glendale Zoo." Darlene read the sign aloud, feeling a ripple of excitement travel up her spine.

What a summer it was going to be! Not only was it her first summer driving, it was also the summer of her first real job. And the job was the best part. Darlene was going to work with baby animals in the zoo nursery.

She still couldn't believe she'd been lucky enough to get the job. A month earlier, Darlene's guidance counselor had called her into

the office and told her that the zoo was looking for a few kids who would be interested in
working there during the summer. The guidance counselor had remembered how much
Darlene loved animals and wanted to know if
she'd be interested.

Interested? Darlene had been thrilled with
the idea. But as the weeks passed and school
ended, Darlene didn't hear any more about the
job. And just as she had lost hope, a letter
came from the zoo asking her to come in for
an interview. At the end of that interview with
the head zookeeper, Darlene had been hired.

Sitting in her car, gazing at the imposing
gates before her, Darlene became as nervous
as she was excited. She had attended an orientation session about a week ago, so she
felt somewhat prepared. But caring for baby
animals is a big responsibility; she hoped
she wouldn't do anything wrong.

Darlene was not only nervous about the
job, she wanted especially to fit in and make
new friends, and this only added to the anxi-
ety she already felt. She took a deep breath
and silently prayed that everything would go
smoothly.

At the orientation, everyone had been told

to wear jeans and a T-shirt, so Darlene wore a brand-new pair of jeans and a short-sleeved T-shirt that was the same golden-green color as her eyes. But as usual, she wasn't satisfied with her hair. Shoulder-length and naturally curly at the ends, Darlene's brown hair seemed to have a mind of its own and never did what she wanted it to do. She fluffed the ends and opened the car door.

As she got out of the car, she sniffed the air, rich with different aromas. A mixture of fresh hay, roasted peanuts, popcorn, and the musky smell of the animals filled her senses. As Darlene approached the gates, she could hear the faint, distant trumpeting of an elephant. The strange sound caused goose bumps to rise on her arms.

"You're new this year," the uniformed guard said, smiling, as she showed him her official employee ID badge.

Darlene nodded, smiling too. "Yes, this is my first summer here. Actually, it's my first job," she confessed.

"I've been here twenty years," the guard told her. "It doesn't pay all that great, but I love the atmosphere." He winked at her from under bushy white eyebrows. "Where else can you have your coffee break with a bunch of monkeys and eat lunch next to a den of lions?"

"That's true." Darlene laughed. The old man's friendliness eased her nerves. "I'm Darlene Sullivan."

"My name's Gus, and I hope you have a wonderful first day on the job."

"Thanks, Gus. I'm sure I will!" She smiled, then passed through the gate and followed the signs pointing to the zoo nursery.

The nursery was close to the area where the big cats were, and as Darlene got closer, she could hear the growls of the tigers and the rumbling complaints of the lions. Although the huge cats fascinated her, they also scared her. She was glad she wasn't working with *them*.

When Darlene stepped inside the glass-windowed building, she immediately smelled an antiseptic scent that reminded her of a hospital. In fact, the zoo nursery closely resembled a hospital nursery for human babies—only inside one of the incubators was a tiny spider monkey. A young chimpanzee chattered at her from his playpen. His long, slender fingers poked through the holes of the screen that covered the top of the pen.

4

"Hi, little fellow," Darlene said, moving closer to the playpen and smiling at the bright, inquisitive expression on the chimpanzee's face.

"Don't let Skeeter's innocent act fool you. He's a real little stinker."

Darlene looked up and smiled at the tall blonde who had just spoken. She looked to be about twenty years old, and she was cradling a baby bear in her arms. "Are you Darlene?" the girl asked.

Darlene nodded.

"I'm Ellen Jordan. Let me put this little critter back where he belongs and then I'll show you around."

Darlene watched with interest as Ellen put the bear cub into a cage and carefully locked the door. She then grabbed a bright-blue smock from a hook on the wall and handed it to Darlene. "This will help keep you clean. The animals aren't always considerate of clothing!" As Darlene put on the smock and buttoned it up, Ellen went on, "Have you ever worked with animals before?"

"Only the ones I've got at home." Darlene grinned. "My parents always complain that I'm trying to start my own zoo."

Ellen laughed. "How many animals do you have?"

"Two birds, four hamsters, a dog, a cat, and a gerbil."

"You remind me of myself a few years ago," Ellen said. "But since then I've discovered something much more interesting."

"What's that?" Darlene asked curiously.

Ellen laughed. "Guys!"

"Not me," Darlene stated firmly. "I promised myself that I'm not going to even look at any boys all summer. I'm devoting myself to my job."

"Uh-oh—sounds like you've had a bad experience," Ellen said.

"Not *one* bad experience, a whole bunch of them," Darlene replied, thinking back to her last several dates. For one reason or another, they all had been catastrophic. "So I decided to keep my life uncomplicated this summer and not date."

"Personally, I like the complication of a guy in my life, especially a certain veterinarian's assistant here at the zoo." Ellen looked down at her wristwatch. "In fact, I'm supposed to meet him at ten o'clock, so let me get you acquainted with everything."

For the next twenty minutes, Ellen showed Darlene around the nursery and explained what her duties would be. There were schedules of feedings posted on the wall, different formulas for different animals, and a refrigerator stocked with all kinds of strange foods and bottles marked with numbers.

The chimp, the monkeys, and the bear cub were not the only animals in the nursery. In a small pool, two baby hippopotamuses "sunned" themselves beneath artificial lights. In a cage was a raccoon who kept trying to pick the lock on his door.

"Actually, this nursery is more like an orphanage," Ellen explained. "We get the babies whose mothers can't or won't care for them. Of course, if it's at all possible, the zoo staff tries to keep the babies with the mothers in as natural a habitat as possible." She paused by the incubator that held the spider monkey. "But sometimes nature needs some help, like with this little guy. He was born prematurely and needed more care than his mother could give him. If we hadn't taken over, he would have died."

Darlene looked at Ellen with a touch of awe. She seemed so knowledgeable about everything. "How long have you been working here?"

"Six years, ever since I was sixteen." Ellen smiled, obviously sensing Darlene's lack of confidence. "Don't worry. It won't be long before you catch on to everything. One of the most important things to remember is to play to our audience." She pointed to the windows. "At feeding times, people gather out there to watch. Make sure you feed the animals close to the window and hold them up so everyone can see. Relax—after a couple of days you'll see how easy it all is." She glanced at her watch again. "I've got to go meet Greg. I'll be back in about fifteen minutes or so. Under the cabinet is a bottle of cleaner and some paper towels—while I'm gone, you can wipe down the countertops and cabinets."

"Wait . . ." Darlene said with a touch of panic. Her head was reeling with information but Ellen was already out the door.

Darlene went over to the cabinet and found the bottle of spray cleaner and the roll of towels. *Please, please don't let anything go wrong while Ellen is away!* she prayed silently.

After she finished wiping down the count-

8

ertops, she went back to the incubator and peered at the spider monkey. He was sleeping on his back, his reddish-gold chest heaving with short, rapid breaths. "Poor little thing," Darlene murmured, wishing she could pick him up and cuddle him close.

She jumped as she heard the excited chatter of the chimpanzee, and looked over at the playpen. Her eyes widened in horror. The playpen was empty; the screen on the top was pushed to one side. The chimp was gone!

Darlene looked around frantically and finally spied him sitting on top of the refrigerator. The expression on his face made him look as if he was laughing at her.

"Ellen's right—you *are* a little stinker," Darlene said, advancing toward him slowly. "How'd you get out of your pen?" He chattered some more, as if answering her question. "That's right, just keep talking to me and stay right where you are," she said gently, getting closer and closer to him. But as she reached up to grab him, Skeeter jumped from the top of the refrigerator to the top of one of the cages, making the bear cub growl in agitation. The raccoon began running around in circles.

"Come on, Skeeter. You're upsetting all the other animals," she begged. But Skeeter only jumped up and down, slapping his hands on the tops of the cages.

He was too high for Darlene to reach, so she grabbed a chair and pulled it up in front of the cages, the whole time speaking calmly in hopes of settling the chimp down. She climbed up on the chair and lunged at him, but the chimp was as quick as greased lightning. In the blink of an eye, he jumped over Darlene's head to a shelf high above her. As she watched him, he opened a cabinet door and pulled out a box of cotton balls, spilling them all over the floor.

Darlene closed her eyes for a moment, feeling the sting of tears of frustration. *I'm going to get fired*, she thought dismally. *My very first day on the job and I'm going to get fired!*

In desperation, Darlene ran to the refrigerator, hoping to find something that she could use to bribe the chimp back to his pen. Her eyes lit up when she saw a couple of bananas on the bottom shelf. She grabbed one and held it out to Skeeter, who was now sitting on top of a cage again.

"Look what I have here." She waved the banana in front of Skeeter, who appeared uninterested. "Hey, look—it's a nice, ripe banana, see?" She peeled it and took a bite. "Mmm! It's such a *good* banana." She took another bite to prove to the chimp how delicious the banana was.

"Would you like a glass of milk to go with that?"

Darlene turned to see a boy about her age standing just inside the door, his brown eyes lit with amusement.

She tried to swallow the lump of banana in her mouth, choking as it got stuck in her throat.

"Hey, are you okay?" The boy moved over to her, clapping her on the back as she coughed.

"No, I'm *not* okay," Darlene finally managed to sputter. She pointed to the chimp, who was grinning down at them from the top of the cages. "He escaped, and he's wrecking the place, and if I don't get him back in his cage before Ellen gets back, I'll probably be fired." She realized that her voice was trembling with emotion and again she felt tears filling her eyes.

11

"Don't get upset, nobody's going to fire you." He smiled at her, showing even, white teeth. "That little monster escapes at least twice a day. I'll get him for you." He moved the chair over to the cages, stood on the chair, and eyed the grinning chimp. "Okay, Skeeter, you've caused enough trouble for one day. Come here." The tone of his voice was low and firm, and to Darlene's astonishment the chimp went right over to him, wrapping long, hairy arms around the boy's neck. He climbed down from the chair. "Skeeter and I are old friends," he told her. "I visit him every day."

Darlene watched as the boy put Skeeter back in the pen and she noticed his long legs and broad shoulders. He was really very good-looking, Darlene thought, with his bold features and friendly smile. He was definitely the type who always attracted her. . . .

Remember, you've sworn off boys for the summer, she told herself firmly. Still, she felt her toes curl up inside her sneakers when he turned around and their eyes met.

Chapter Two

"There—he's safe and sound," the boy said, flashing his gorgeous grin.

Darlene smiled back. "Thanks a lot!"

"I'm Aaron Caldwell," the boy said. "Who are you?"

"I'm Darlene . . . Darlene Sullivan," she answered shyly.

"Well, Darlene Sullivan, if you don't want anyone to know about Skeeter's little escape trick, we'd better pick up all those cotton balls." Aaron pointed to the white cotton puffs that dotted the floor.

"Oh, that's okay—I can get them. You did enough by just catching the little guy. I really appreciate your help. I don't think I would ever have gotten him down. Thanks for all your help, Aaron, and it was nice meeting you," she said, turning abruptly away from him and bending to pick up the cotton balls. There was really no point in getting to know him better. Her summer plans definitely did *not* include a guy, even if he did have eyes the color of dark caramels and a warm smile. As she busied herself, Darlene became aware of Aaron's gaze following her curiously.

"Yeah, it was nice meeting you, too, Darlene," he finally said, heading for the door. "I guess I'll be seeing you around."

"Right—be seeing you," Darlene replied with a friendly smile. She waited until he was gone, then let out a sigh of relief and hurried over to the plate glass window to watch him walk away. She liked the way he walked, with his shoulders back and his head held high, confident and self-assured.

After a few minutes, she turned away from the window and scowled. She couldn't become interested in Aaron Caldwell! Over the last year, Darlene had had more awful dates than she could endure. It wasn't that the guys she went out with were so bad—most of them had been perfectly nice. But weird circumstances had ruined every single date.

With Tommy Oakes, shrimp had screwed up the night. They had gone to a seafood restaurant and Darlene had eaten shrimp. Their date had ended abruptly when she suffered an allergic reaction and Tommy had to rush her to the emergency room. Then there had been the time she spent the whole evening complaining about how mean Mrs. Jackson, her math teacher, was, only to discover that Mrs. Jackson was her date's favorite aunt.

"Hi, I'm back. Did everything go okay?" Ellen breezed through the door, and Darlene pushed all thoughts of dating and Aaron Caldwell out of her mind. The rest of the morning was filled with so many new experiences that Darlene didn't have time to think of anything other than her job.

At ten-thirty a crowd began to gather in front of the windows, and Ellen took the baby spider monkey out of the incubator.

"You want to feed him?" Ellen asked, wrapping him up in a little blue blanket. "He just gets a bottle."

"Sure." Darlene took the monkey in her arms, and Ellen handed her a bottle filled with formula. His little face peered up at her expectantly as Darlene moved closer to the window and held the bottle to his mouth. His tiny hands reached up to grasp it, and the baby monkey drank greedily.

Darlene felt a thrill of excitement race through her. This was what her job was all about, helping baby animals who needed her. It was wonderful to look down at the monkey and see his brown eyes gazing at her trustingly. Who needed guys or dates? Her summer was going to be just fine without them.

At noon, when it was time to take her lunch break, Darlene reluctantly left the nursery. Ellen had told her that most of the kids ate lunch at a nearby concession stand, so that was where she headed.

She had no trouble finding the stand, a thatch-roofed hut that looked like it belonged in an African village. Even if she hadn't been able to see it, her nose would have led her to the scents of plump, juicy hot dogs, popcorn, soft pretzels, and cotton candy.

As she approached, Darlene saw girls wearing zoo smocks like hers, tourists, and other zoo employees sitting at tables beneath color-ful umbrellas. Darlene ordered a hot dog, a bag of potato chips, and a root beer. As she looked for a place to sit, Darlene noticed one of the girls motioning to her.

"Come on over here and sit with us," the girl called.

With a shy smile, Darlene approached the four girls at the table. The dark-haired girl who had called to her moved over to make room for Darlene. "Hi, I'm Alysia Walker," she said, smiling.

"Thanks. I'm Darlene Sullivan."

"You're new, right?" Alysia asked.

Darlene nodded. "Today's my first day."

"Meet Chrissy, Amy, and Kate."

"So, where did they stick you?" Kate asked, flipping a strand of long blond hair over her shoulder.

"I'm working in the nursery," Darlene answered.

"Ugh, what a drag!" Kate grimaced.

Laughing, Alysia said, "Oh, don't mind her. Kate's in a bad mood because she got stuck selling souvenirs in the kiddie petting farm."

"Well, I think working in the nursery

sounds terrific," Amy said, ignoring Kate. "All those cute little baby animals must be a lot of fun to work with."

Darlene nodded. "They are, but there's so much to learn."

"You'll catch on to everything real fast," Alysia said. "We all did. This is Kate's third summer here, and the second year for the rest of us." She smiled at Darlene reassuringly. "Don't worry, before long you'll be a veteran, too." Alysia seemed to be going out of her way to make Darlene feel welcome, and Darlene appreciated it.

"I hear we're getting a new elephant," Chrissy said, changing the subject.

"I heard the same thing. Anyone want my apple?" Amy held out the piece of fruit to the other girls.

"I'll take it if nobody else wants it," Chrissy said. "I'll cut it up and give it to Candy Cane."

"Chrissy takes care of the grounds where the zebras are. She's named one of them Candy Cane and she's trying to train it to eat out of her hand," Alysia explained to Darlene.

"Doc Rockwell says Chelsea is going to

have her cubs in the next couple of weeks," Amy said, finishing the last of her hot dog.

"Doc Rockwell is the zoo veterinarian, and Chelsea is a tigress," Alysia told Darlene, then giggled. "I feel like a translator!"

"Hi, Darlene . . . ladies." They all turned to see Aaron approaching, his gaze focused on Darlene. "Did our little Houdini cause you any more problems this morning?" he asked her.

She smiled and shook her head, realizing that his eyes weren't really brown. Instead they were a warm shade of hazel. "No problems at all. Skeeter has behaved very well since his escape." She was aware of the other girls' eyes on her and she felt her cheeks burning.

"If you ever need any help with him, don't hesitate to holler. I'll be glad to give you a hand."

Darlene nodded. "Thanks. I'll keep that in mind."

"Well, I'd better go grab some lunch. I'll see you later." Aaron turned and walked over to the concession hut.

"I can't *believe* you!" Chrissy squealed,

staring at Darlene in astonishment. "On your first day here you have the biggest hunk around offering to help you!"

"Well, enjoy his attention while it lasts," Kate said dryly. " 'Cause with Aaron it never lasts long."

"What do you mean?" Darlene asked.

"Several of us have been out with Aaron once or twice, but he never dates anyone more often than that," Kate explained.

"Yeah, but I think I can safely say that any of us would jump at the chance to go out with him again. He's a really nice guy," Amy added, and Darlene couldn't help but nod in agreement.

"I see you made it though your first day," Gus, the guard, said as Darlene passed through the gate on her way home.

"Yes, and I didn't foul anything up too badly either!" Darlene laughed. "See you tomorrow, Gus."

"Okay, little lady. See you in the morning." Gus tipped his hat, exposing his pink, bald head.

Darlene had just reached her car when she

heard somebody call her name. Looking up, she saw Alysia hurrying toward her.

"How'd your first day go?" Alysia asked.

"Great," Darlene replied. "I know I'm going to love working here."

"Good. I didn't get a chance to ask you at lunch—where do you go to school?"

"North High. I'm going to be a junior."

"Me, too. Only I go to South High." Alysia leaned back against Darlene's car. "Maybe some night after work we could get together for a pizza or something."

"Sure, I'd like that," Darlene agreed, realizing she'd like to become friends with the cute, lively girl. Darlene's best friend, Julie, had moved away a month ago, and she missed having a special friend around.

"Great! Maybe we can plan something later in the week. I'd better go. Monday is my night to cook dinner. I'll see you tomorrow." Alysia waved at Darlene and headed for her own car.

What a day! Darlene thought as she drove home. She'd fed a spider monkey, learned how to groom a bear cub, and met a girl she hoped would become a good friend. She tried not to think about what Aaron might become.

That evening over dinner, Darlene told her parents and Kevin, her six-year-old brother, about her day.

"Wow, you got to feed a spider?" Kevin said.

"Not a spider, Kev. A spider *monkey*. They like to hang upside down in trees, and when they do, they look like spiders," Darlene explained. "I held him in my arms and gave him a bottle just like a real baby."

"Awesome! How did it feel?" he asked, his brown eyes wide.

Darlene thought for a moment. "Actually, it reminded me of when I was ten years old and Mom let me hold you for the first time." She laughed at her brother's look of outrage. "Just kidding, Kev."

"I don't know if I like the idea of you working with bear cubs. That sounds dangerous," Mrs. Sullivan said, her forehead wrinkled with worry.

"Ellen made me wear gloves today when I groomed the cub," Darlene told her. "Besides, it's really not dangerous at all. The animals in the nursery have all been born in captivity. They really aren't like wild animals. Ellen has been working in the nursery for six years and she's never been scratched or bitten."

"Mom, will you take me to visit the zoo one day so we can see Darlene working?" Kevin asked.

"Sure, that sounds like fun," Mrs. Sullivan said.

"I might even take a day off and go with you," Mr. Sullivan offered, grinning at Darlene. "It's not every day I get to see my girl caring for wild beasts. Although some of the dates she's brought home have resembled . . ."

"*Dad!*" Darlene interrupted, giggling. "Anyway, I think it's going to be a great summer."

After dinner, Darlene went into her bedroom. She fed her hamsters and her two parakeets, then lay down on her bed, exhausted by the day's activities and all the excitement of her new job.

Funny—when she'd told her family about the chimp escaping she hadn't even mentioned Aaron Caldwell. She'd simply told them that someone had helped her get Skeeter back into his pen.

He's just another zoo worker, she told herself. *So what if he has a smile that could melt an ice cube? So what if his eyes are the nicest shade of hazel I've ever seen?*

Then she thought about what the other girls had said about Aaron, how he never dated a girl more than once or twice. If he ever asked her out, she certainly wasn't about to break her "no dating" policy for a guy like that!

Still, as she closed her eyes, she wondered why it was that every time he'd smiled at her, her stomach had felt all jumpy and strange. Maybe she was ill. That had to be it! She was coming down with the flu—or something.

Chapter Three

Alysia ran across the parking lot the following morning to catch up with Darlene. "I can't believe it's only June. It's so hot," Alysia said, brushing her dark hair back from her forehead.

"I heard it's supposed to get even warmer by the end of the week," Darlene said as Alysia fell into step beside her.

"Bummer," Alysia said, then brightened. "Hey, you ever go to the Wingate pool?"

"Sometimes," Darlene answered after a brief pause. She wasn't about to admit that she didn't know how to swim.

"Great! Why don't we make plans to go swimming this Saturday?" Alysia suggested.

Darlene hesitated again before answering. She certainly didn't want to go to the pool, but she didn't want Alysia to know the reason. "Sure, that sounds like fun," she finally said. She figured that she could work on her tan. She didn't have to actually go *in* the water.

"Good, we'll make final plans later in the week. I'll see you at lunch." Alysia waved and the two girls parted ways.

"Oh good, I'm so glad you're here," Ellen said the minute Darlene walked in the door the next morning. "I told Greg I'd meet him first thing this morning. Can you keep an eye on things while I'm gone? The babies have all had breakfast." She removed her smock and patted her blond hair into place.

"Uh—okay," Darlene answered uncertainly. She really didn't like being left alone in the nursery. If anything went wrong with one of the animals the way it had yesterday, she wasn't sure she'd know what to do. But Ellen was her boss and Darlene didn't want to make her think that she couldn't cope.

"Don't worry, I won't be long," Ellen said as she ran out.

The first thing Darlene did was check to make sure the top of Skeeter's pen was securely fastened. She didn't want a repeat performance of yesterday's escape. After that, she pulled up a stool next to the incubator, watching the spider monkey sleep. He looked so little and helpless. She wondered if he missed his mother and if he got lonely for other monkeys. He was lucky to be born in a zoo, where skilled workers could ensure him a long and healthy life. If he'd been born in the wild, he probably wouldn't have lived very long.

Darlene turned her attention to the door to see Aaron standing there. All the symptoms she'd written off the night before as the flu came rushing back. Her stomach tied itself into a knot, and as Aaron smiled, she felt hot and cold at the same time. "Oh, hi," she said, noticing how the color of his dark green T-shirt was reflected in his eyes, making them appear the color of a deep, dark forest.

Aaron pulled up a stool and sat down next to Darlene. She could immediately smell his after-shave, a spicy scent that blended with the fresh, clean scent of his shirt. "How's he doing?" he asked, looking down at the sleeping animal.

"He seems to be doing fine. But he sleeps an awful lot."

Aaron nodded. "That's because he was premature. It won't be long before he'll be driving you crazy trying to get out of his incubator."

"Like his buddy over there." Darlene grinned and pointed to Skeeter, who was playing with baby blocks in his pen.

Aaron laughed. "He looks almost human, doesn't he?"

"I think monkeys are fascinating," Darlene said. "When I was little and we'd visit the zoo, they were always my favorites. Then I went through an elephant stage and a giraffe phase." She laughed self-consciously, realizing she was rambling. "I guess I just love all animals," she finished.

"That's the way I feel," he agreed. "I love them all, but I've always had this special feeling for tigers. They seem so noble and aloof. That's what I do here—work with the lions and tigers."

"Isn't that sort of scary?" Darlene's eyes widened.

"Not really. My supervisor doesn't let me do anything that could be considered dangerous. Besides, the lions and tigers who have been born and raised in zoos are much more docile than ones in the wild." He frowned for a moment, then continued. "Tigers have gotten a bad reputation as being vicious man-eaters, but the truth is they're actually very shy and try to avoid contact with people."

"I heard yesterday that one of the tigers is going to have cubs." Darlene was impressed by Aaron's knowledge.

"Yeah, that's Chelsea. She's my favorite." It was obvious by the expression on Aaron's face that he loved talking about tigers. "Chelsea was just a cub herself when I first started working here. She seemed to take to me, so I started spending a lot of extra time with her. Now she's three and a half years old and she and I are special buddies." He paused and smiled with a charming touch of embarrassment. "Sorry, I didn't mean to bore you with tiger stories."

"You aren't boring me," Darlene said

quickly. "I think it all sounds fascinating." It was true—she was finding everything about Aaron fascinating, and that disturbed her. Why did he have to be so nice and interesting? Why did she keep feeling as if she were falling into his beautiful, changeable eyes?

"I'd better get busy," she said suddenly, getting up from her stool. She didn't like the direction of her thoughts. "Yesterday Ellen showed me how to mix the formula and fix the bottles for the rest of the day. I'd better start doing it." She grabbed a can of formula from one of the cabinets. "Do you want me to tell Ellen you stopped by?"

Aaron shook his head. "No, I didn't stop by to talk to Ellen."

"Oh," Darlene replied, not knowing what else to say.

"I stopped by to see you."

"Oh?" Darlene repeated, her heart lurching in her chest.

"Seeing you yesterday morning just sort of started my day off on the right foot, so I decided to do the same thing this morning," Aaron said with a grin. "But now I'd better get back to work, too. I'll see you later." His warm, attractive smile made Darlene's stomach feel funny again.

After he left the nursery, Darlene realized that she'd really enjoyed talking to Aaron. She wanted to get to know him better, but she didn't want to ruin everything by going out with him.

She decided that it would be nice to be friends with Aaron. After all, Darlene had several friends who were boys. She enjoyed talking to them and hanging out with them, and there was absolutely nothing romantic about it. But the only thing that worried her was the fact that none of those other friends tied her stomach in knots, made her toes curl, and made her palms sweat. None of them made her feel all hot and cold and shy and tongue-tied. What was so different about Aaron Caldwell?

Ellen sent Darlene to lunch late, so Darlene found herself eating alone at one of the tables near the concession hut. She smiled as a family passed by. A little girl tugged on her mother's hand, begging to see the monkeys.

Some of Darlene's happiest memories were

associated with the zoo. Her family had always made a point of visiting it several times each summer. Glendale, Kansas, was a small town and the zoo was a major attraction—not only for the families who lived there, but for those in the surrounding counties as well.

Darlene bit into her hot dog and wondered why hot dogs at the zoo always tasted better than the ones cooked at home. She looked up and to her surprise saw Aaron coming toward her, holding a hot dog, a bag of potato chips, and a can of soda. He slid into the seat across from her. "You're eating lunch late today," he observed.

She nodded, quickly swallowing her last bite. "We had a lot of visitors around noon, so Ellen asked me to wait a little while for lunch."

"I'm glad she did. This way we can eat lunch together." Aaron smiled and leaned forward, touching a paper napkin to her chin. "Ketchup," he explained.

"Thanks," Darlene murmured, knowing her face was probably as red as the ketchup that had been on her chin.

"Tell me something about yourself," Aaron

said between bites. "What do you like to do when you're not working here at the zoo?"

He had a way of looking at her and smiling that made Darlene feel that she was the most important person in the world. She felt her blush deepen as she shrugged and murmured, "The usual things." At the moment she couldn't seem to think of one single thing she liked to do. All she could think of was how his hair shone in the afternoon sunshine and how he had a little cleft in his chin she hadn't noticed before.

"Alysia told me you're going to be a junior at North High next year. I'm going to be a senior at South, then I'm going to college to study zoology," Aaron said. "I'm going to be a vet."

"That sounds great! I think I want to be a vet, too," Darlene replied.

"Does that mean you took this job just because you love animals?" His eyes twinkled with amusement. "From what I hear, most of the girls work here for the opportunity to meet guys."

Darlene stuck out her chin. "Not me. I'm here to learn more about animals," she said firmly, then eyed him with a smile. "What about you? Are you working here because *you* love animals or because you want to meet girls?"

Aaron laughed. "I love the animals, but I've met some nice girls here, too. In fact, I've made a lot of good friends." He opened the bag of potato chips and offered it to her.

Darlene shook her head. "How's Chelsea doing?" she asked.

Aaron beamed. "She's doing great. You should come over to the cat area and let me introduce her to you."

"I'd like that," Darlene said with a shy smile. No problem there. She wasn't agreeing to go out with him—she was only agreeing to meet his favorite tigress. "I guess everyone's really excited about her having cubs."

"Yeah, they haven't had a lot of success breeding the tigers until Chelsea mated with Winston." He paused to take a few more bites of his hot dog. "Why do you suppose the hot dogs here always taste so much better than the ones my mom makes at home?"

"I was just wondering that before," Darlene said, laughing. She was thrilled that she and Aaron were on the same wavelength.

"You were?" He smiled, as if he, too, was

pleased by them sharing a thought. For a long moment their gazes met and held. "I love junk food," he continued when Darlene tore her eyes from his. "Give me a hot dog over a steak any day of the week."

"My favorites are pizza and tacos," Darlene confessed. "And nachos smothered with cheese."

"Ah, a girl after my own heart." He was teasing, but the expression in his eyes made a shiver dance up and down Darlene's spine. He leaned closer to her across the table. "Do all the Sullivan girls have gorgeous eyes and pretty smiles like yours?"

"There aren't any other Sullivan girls in my family," Darlene answered, blushing. "I have a six-year-old brother, but that's it." Darlene wondered if Aaron could hear her heart beating a mile a minute in her chest.

"Are you seeing anyone, dating anyone special?" he asked casually.

She shook her head slowly. Was he going to ask her out? It certainly sounded like that was what he was leading up to, and Darlene didn't know what she was going to do if he did. She actually would *love* to go out with him. He was so nice looking and he seemed like he would be a lot of fun. But on the other hand, she was afraid of doing something so embarrassing that he wouldn't even want to be her friend.

Aaron suddenly glanced at his watch. "Wow, I've got to get back," he said. He wadded up his trash and threw it into a nearby basket. "I'm glad we got to eat lunch together." He got up from the table. "See you later."

" 'Bye." Darlene watched him walk away, knowing she should be relieved. She had been so sure he was going to ask her out and she was confused about how to respond. Yes, she *should* be relieved. Then why did she feel so disappointed?

Chapter Four

"I told Chelsea that a cute brunette was coming to visit her this evening and she had to be on her best behavior," Aaron said the following day. He had caught up with Darlene as she was getting ready to leave and he had talked her into visiting the tigress that afternoon. "She spent the whole afternoon cleaning her coat, getting ready for you."

Darlene laughed. "Just as long as she didn't spend the afternoon sharpening her teeth and claws."

"It wouldn't matter if she had. She's in a cage behind bars." Aaron frowned and Darlene thought he was going to say something

37

else, but instead he grabbed her hand and quickened their pace.

Darlene liked the way his hand felt enclosing hers. It made her feel warm and wonderful. Of course, she reminded herself, just because she was holding Aaron's hand and going with him to see his favorite tigress didn't mean she was going back on her "no romance" policy.

When she felt her heart pounding rapidly, she wasn't sure whether it was because Aaron was holding her hand or because they had reached a cage where a huge lion was pacing back and forth. As they paused in front of the large cage, the lion let out a loud roar.

"That's Sultan," Aaron explained. "He's seven years old."

Darlene was amazed by his size. "He's so *big!*"

"His mane makes him look bigger than he really is. Actually, he's small as lions go. Sultan only weighs three hundred and twenty-five pounds, but some lions weigh as much as five hundred pounds."

Darlene shivered. "Three hundred and

twenty-five or five hundred pounds, I'm glad there are bars between him and me!"

Aaron squeezed her hand and smiled at her. "Don't worry. I'll make sure nothing happens to you."

And as Darlene looked into his hazel eyes, she believed him. She had all the faith in the world that Aaron would protect her.

"Come on." He pulled her forward. "I want you to see all the cats before I introduce you to Chelsea."

Aaron showed her the cheetahs and jaguars, the leopards and ocelots. He knew all of them by name and spouted enough information about each one to fill volumes of books. It was funny, Darlene thought. If it had been her dad telling her about natural habitats, she probably would have been bored stiff. But when Aaron talked about them, she was utterly fascinated.

"It's hard to believe that people actually kill these animals just so somebody can have a fur coat," Darlene said as they stood in front of a beautiful spotted leopard's cage.

"Well, times are changing and people are becoming more aware of animal rights."

Aaron scowled. "It's just a shame that there are some people who will always put their vanity above the rights of other living creatures." His frown was replaced with a huge smile as he led Darlene to another cage. A beautiful tigress, with rich golden fur and black stripes, lay there sleeping.

"And now, here's Chelsea. Chelsea? Hey, girl," Aaron called to the tigress, who opened one golden eye to look at him lazily. "Look, I've brought the cute brunette I was telling you about. This is Darlene."

Darlene blushed at his words, then watched as the pregnant tigress rose to her feet, came over to the bars in front of the cage and rubbed against them, just like a big house cat. Aaron ducked under the large wooden bar that was meant to keep the public from coming too close to the cage. "Come on, it's okay," he urged when she hesitated.

Reluctantly, Darlene followed him beneath the wooden bar, but hung back when he went right up to the cage. She watched in amazement as Aaron reached in and scratched the tigress behind her ears.

"She certainly is friendly, isn't she?" Darlene said.

"Yeah, Chelsea loves people," Aaron replied, laughing as the big cat licked his hand. "You want to pet her?"

Darlene shook her head vigorously. She had to admit Chelsea *looked* tame enough, but she wasn't quite ready to stick her hand into a tiger's cage.

"Maybe another time," Aaron said, and Darlene was grateful that he didn't seem to think she was a coward.

"She's beautiful," Darlene said, smiling at Aaron.

"She is, isn't she?" Aaron agreed proudly, as if he had been personally responsible for creating the creature. "And her cubs are going to be beautiful, too." He gave Chelsea a farewell pat before he and Darlene began to walk back toward the main gate of the zoo.

"So, what do you do all day when you're working with the cats?" Darlene asked.

"I'm teaching the lions to jump through hoops of fire and the ocelots to catch Frisbees," Aaron said solemnly, reaching out to take her hand once again.

Darlene looked at him suspiciously. "You're putting me on, right?" She grinned as she saw the teasing glint in his eyes.

41

Aaron laughed. "Actually, the truth is I spend most of my days carrying feed and cleaning out cages. It's really kind of a dull job. You have to admit, teaching ocelots to catch Frisbees sounds a lot more exciting than the truth. Well, here we are," he said as they stopped beside her car.

"Thanks for introducing me to Chelsea," Darlene said. "She's really neat."

"I'm glad you liked her. She's very special to me." His smile made Darlene's stomach do funny things. "I'll see you in the morning." He reached out and gave her hand a quick squeeze, then took off in the direction of his own car.

Darlene watched him go, torn by conflicting emotions. She was relieved that Aaron hadn't asked her for a date, but again, she was disappointed. Why hadn't he asked her out? He seemed to go out of his way to see her. He'd introduced her to his favorite tigress. He'd even flirted with her several times. So why hadn't he asked her out? Was something wrong with her?

"I just don't understand it," Darlene said to Alysia. It was Saturday afternoon and the two girls were lying on lounge chairs near the edge of the Wingate pool. Although Darlene had been reluctant to come, she'd wanted to spend more time with Alysia. "Aaron really acts like he's interested in me, but he hasn't asked me out." Darlene pushed her sunglasses up on the top of her head and sighed. "I'm beginning to think he never will."

"But if he does, are you still going to turn him down?" Alysia asked. Darlene had told her about her "no dating" policy.

"I don't know if I'd turn Aaron down or not. I really want to go out with him, but I'm afraid I'll do something dumb that will wreck everything," she confessed.

"What do you mean? What could you possibly do that would be that bad?" Alysia asked, screwing the lid back on her bottle of oil.

"If we went to play miniature golf, I'd probably bean him with a golf ball. If we went bowling, I'd probably drop the bowling ball on his foot. If we went out to eat, I'd spill something either on him or on me." Darlene sighed again. "Dates and I just don't seem to mix," she finished sadly.

"You sound like an accident waiting to

happen," Alysia teased. "But just because those kinds of things happened before doesn't mean they'd happen with Aaron."

"I know, but I'm afraid to risk it," Darlene said. "Right now, everything's cool. I look forward to him coming into the nursery to see me, and sometimes we eat lunch together. Lately, he's been flirting with me a lot." Darlene felt her cheeks grow warm. "I guess I just don't want to go out with him and mess up so badly that he won't even want to be friends with me anymore. Besides, maybe this is for the best. Remember, Kate said that Aaron never dates a girl more than a couple of times. If I don't have an official date with him, maybe he won't get tired of me so fast."

"Personally, I think you're nuts," Alysia said, getting up out of her lounge chair. "In my opinion, if there is one doubt in your mind about dating Aaron, then you need to see a shrink. He's a total fox. Come on, let's take a dip. Maybe some cool water will straighten out your brain."

"You go ahead. I'm really not hot." Actually, she was roasting, but Darlene wasn't ready to admit to Alysia that she didn't know how to swim.

"You sure you don't want to come in?"

Darlene nodded. "Positive. You go ahead." She watched with a mixture of admiration and envy as Alysia climbed up the steps to the high diving board. Waving to Darlene, she executed a perfect dive into the cool blue water below. It would be wonderful to be able to jump right into the water and not have to worry about drowning, Darlene thought.

Darlene jumped as somebody behind her placed their hands over her eyes. "Guess who?" a deep voice said. Before she could reply, the hands were removed and Aaron moved around in front of her.

"Aaron, what are you doing here?" she asked, pleasantly surprised.

"The same thing you are. Trying to find some relief from this heat." He sat down in the empty chair beside her. "How's the water?"

"I don't know. I haven't been in." Darlene blushed as he grinned at her, grateful that she had decided to spend some of her salary on a new bathing suit for her day at the pool with Alysia. She'd chosen a pretty peach two-piece, one she knew complemented her brown hair and eyes.

"You look terrific in that color," he observed.

"You don't look so bad yourself," Darlene returned with a flirtatious smile. It was true—Aaron looked great in his swim trunks. And he had a wonderful all-over tan. "Do you come here often?" she asked.

"Every weekend. My family has a summer pass here. What about you? How come I've never seen you here before?" He looked at her curiously.

"I don't come very often. Alysia talked me into coming today." She pointed to her friend, who was back up on the high diving board.

"Oh yeah? Alysia's really a good swimmer." He stood up suddenly and held out his hand to Darlene. "Come on and swim with me."

"Oh, no," Darlene said quickly. "I'm enjoying the sun." She wished she could reach out and take his hand and dive into the pool with him! It would be great to swim next to him, shoulder to shoulder. But that was just a pleasant fantasy. The reality was that she couldn't swim. "You go ahead. I'll just sit here and watch," she said. "I really want to work on my tan."

"Maybe you just need a little encouragement," he teased. "Maybe I should just pick you up and throw you in."

"*No!*" Darlene couldn't keep the panic out of her voice.

"Hey, I was just kidding," Aaron said quickly, kneeling down beside her. "I'd never throw anyone into a pool." He took her hand in his. "Really, I was just joking. If you don't want to swim with me, it's no big deal."

"It's not that," Darlene said, not wanting him to think she didn't want to swim with him. She took a deep breath. "The problem is—I can't."

He frowned, obviously not understanding what she was saying. "What do you mean, you can't?"

Darlene sighed. "Just what I said." She looked at him seriously. "I don't know how to swim," she confessed hesitantly. He stared at her for a long moment, as if he were unable to believe what he had just heard.

"You don't know how to swim?" he asked incredulously.

Darlene nodded numbly. *That does it*, she thought miserably. She stared at the water in the pool, waiting for the sound of Aaron's laughter.

Chapter Five

"Hey." Aaron cupped his hand beneath Darlene's chin, making her look at him. "Not being able to swim is nothing to be ashamed of." To her amazement, he didn't sound disgusted and she saw no hint of laughter in his eyes.

"I just feel so dumb," she said, suddenly glad she'd told the truth. "I've never told anyone else," she added shyly. "Not even Alysia knows I can't swim."

"I'm glad you told me. Otherwise I might have thought you didn't want to swim with me because you didn't like me."

"Oh, no, that's not it at all," she hurried

to assure him. "I'd really like to swim with you. I just don't know how."

"I could teach you," he offered.

"Oh, I don't know . . ." Darlene was torn between her desire to spend more time with him and her fear of looking stupid.

"I taught my mom to swim last summer," Aaron said. "She didn't know how, either."

Darlene stared at him in surprise. "Your mother didn't know how to swim?" Somehow this information made her feel less like a freak.

"When Mom was little, she fell into a pool and almost drowned. She's been afraid of the water ever since," Aaron told her. "Finally last year she decided she was tired of being afraid. So she asked me to teach her how to swim and I did. She learned real fast, too." He grinned as if he was proud of his mother's accomplishment, and this only made Darlene like him more. He sobered suddenly. "Did something like that happen to you?"

"No, nothing dramatic like that. I just never learned," she explained. "As I got older, I was too embarrassed to tell anyone or do anything about it."

"Why don't you let me teach you?" Aaron

stood up again and held out his hand. "We'll start by just walking around in the shallow end. It'll be perfectly safe, I promise."

Darlene looked out at the sparkling turquoise pool, then at his hand that was stretched out to her. The water looked so inviting, and she was so hot. "Okay," she agreed, letting him pull her to her feet. Aaron's hand felt warm and secure around hers as they walked over to the steps that led down into the shallow end of the pool.

As they stepped down and the water lapped at their ankles, he tightened his grip on her hand and smiled at her reassuringly. "Don't worry—I promise I won't let go of you."

Darlene smiled back at him, glad that he understood her apprehension. She wasn't terrified, but she was nervous.

They took another step down, and the water level was now up to their thighs. "I didn't realize how hot I was. The water feels so refreshing," Darlene said. Actually, she was thinking how wonderful it was being with Aaron, his hand holding hers. Once again she found herself admiring him, realizing how handsome he was. His dark hair shone, the strands revealing hints of auburn in the bright sunlight, and his hazel eyes were flecked with greenish gold. Darlene noticed that he had freckles across his broad shoulders, and she thought she'd never seen such adorable freckles.

As they stepped down to the floor of the pool, the water rose to their waists, making Darlene gasp. "It's *cold!*" she cried.

"You'll get used to it in a minute. You okay?" he asked.

Darlene nodded, thinking she'd be okay forever if he kept holding her hand.

"See, it's not so bad. Just get used to the way you feel in the water," he suggested.

"I feel really light."

Aaron said, "Now just relax and lift your feet off the bottom for a minute."

She did, for less than a minute, grabbing his shoulder as she started to go under. He laughed and held her up in his strong arms. Darlene quickly put her feet back down, wondering if he could hear her heart beating so quickly.

"You okay?" he asked again, pushing a strand of her wet hair off her forehead. Before Darlene could tell him that she was, she heard Alysia calling to them.

"Hey, you guys!"

They both looked over to see Alysia swimming toward them with long, powerful strokes. "Hi, Aaron," she said, standing up and sweeping her wet hair off her face. "Why don't you and Darlene come out here and swim with me? We could play water tag or something."

Aaron squeezed Darlene's hand and quickly answered, "I really don't feel much like swimming today. I talked Darlene into staying here in the shallow end with me."

"Okay, suit yourselves. Guess I'll get out and catch some more rays." Waving to them, Alysia swam over to the opposite side of the pool where she pulled herself out and began toweling off.

"Thanks—that was a nice thing to do," Darlene said to Aaron.

He shrugged his shoulders and grinned. "I guess I'm just a nice guy."

The rest of the afternoon flew by for Darlene. She and Aaron stayed in the water for a while, then got out and joined Alysia. As they lay in the sun, they all talked about their schools and their families, and Darlene learned a little bit more about Aaron. She

53

found out he had two older sisters, both in college. His dad worked in real estate and his mother was a clerk in a department store.

Alysia told stories about her nine-year-old twin sisters whom she had nicknamed "Rude" and "Crude." "They are totally obnoxious," she insisted. "When *we* were nine years old, we weren't obnoxious, were we?"

"Definitely not!" Darlene laughed.

"No way," Aaron added.

As they laughed, Alysia looked at her wristwatch. "Time flies when you're having fun. We've got to get going soon. I promised Mom I'd be home around four. I'm babysitting the Double-Trouble-Twins tonight." She stood up and began gathering her things.

Darlene stood up too and picked up her towel and purse. "Darlene will meet you at the car," Aaron told Alysia. "I just want to talk to her for a second, okay?"

"Okay," Alysia agreed with a grin and headed off toward the pool exit.

Darlene looked at Aaron expectantly, her heart beating a rapid rhythm. Surely after spending so much time with her today, Aaron was going to invite her out on a real date. And when he did, Darlene knew she was going to say yes. She had had it with her silly no-dating policy!

"I was thinking if you want to meet me here next Saturday, I'll start teaching you how to float and dog-paddle," Aaron said.

"Oh—okay," Darlene agreed, trying to ignore a sharp stab of disappointment. Still, meeting him at the pool was better than nothing. . . .

"Great! Why don't we plan on meeting here about one o'clock next Saturday afternoon?" Aaron suggested.

She nodded. "It's a deal. And thanks for all your help today."

"I enjoyed it," he said with a smile. "You'd better hurry or Alysia might drive off without you."

Darlene nodded again and hurried toward the exit, feeling very confused.

"Well, did he ask you out?" Alysia asked eagerly the minute Darlene got into the car.

"No, but he did ask me to meet him here next Saturday."

"That's almost as good as a date," Alysia replied.

Darlene shook her head. "No, it isn't, but thanks for trying to make me feel better."

She sighed unhappily. "I'm beginning to think there's something terribly wrong with me."

"That's silly," Alysia scoffed, steering the car out of the lot and onto the street. "I know Aaron really likes you. It's so obvious."

"Then why doesn't he ask me out?" Darlene asked.

Alysia grinned at her. "Maybe he's made the same kind of dumb no-dating rule that you did."

"Great," Darlene said sarcastically. "It would be just my luck to fall for a guy who's decided not to date again for the rest of his life!"

Alysia giggled and after a moment Darlene joined her, but somehow she didn't find it very funny.

"Did you have fun at the pool today with Alysia?" Mrs. Sullivan asked as Darlene helped prepare supper that evening.

"Yeah, it was pretty neat."

"I hope you remembered to take some sunscreen," her mother said. "You know too much sun isn't good for you."

Darlene grinned. "Don't worry, Mom. I not only took it, I actually used it."

Her mother looked relieved. "I'm so glad you've made a new friend." She handed Darlene a cucumber to slice for the salad. "I know how much you've missed Julie since she moved away."

"I still miss Julie," Darlene said, "but I really like Alysia. She's a lot of fun."

"It's nice to have special friends. And it's especially nice to have a friend who works at the same place you do," Mrs. Sullivan said, handing her a tomato to add to the salad.

"We ran into somebody else at the pool today who works at the zoo," Darlene said, slicing the tomato. "His name is Aaron Caldwell. He works with the lions and tigers."

"Oh?" Mrs. Sullivan smiled knowingly, her eyebrows raised.

"What are you thinking?" Darlene felt herself blushing.

"Your voice took on a sort of lilt when you said his name. And now your face is bright pink, and *not* from sunburn. Tell me about him."

"Oh Mom, he's *wonderful*!" Darlene answered. She set the rest of the tomato aside and beamed at her mother. "He's great-looking and he has a good sense of humor, and best of all, he's really nice. I like him more than any guy I've ever known!"

Mrs. Sullivan smiled at her. "Sounds good. How does he feel about you?"

Darlene looked away, a frown on her face. "I'm not sure," she admitted. "He acts like he likes me. He seems to go out of his way to talk to me. He's even teaching me how to swim. But he hasn't asked me for a date yet."

"Maybe he's just shy," Mrs. Sullivan suggested. "Boys sometimes are, you know."

"Maybe," Darlene agreed without conviction, and resumed slicing the tomato. There was no way she believed the trouble was that Aaron was shy. He hadn't had any problem asking for dates last summer, according to Kate and Amy.

Chapter Six

Early Monday morning, Darlene held the hose over the small pool of water in the pen where the baby hippopotamuses were housed. The two plump little hippos were lying near the pool, sunning themselves beneath the brilliant artificial light. She laughed as one of them opened his eyes and moved his head, nudging a brightly colored beach ball with his big mouth. The ball shot across the slippery surface and into the water, but the baby hippo just closed his eyes again. "Too lazy to play today, huh?" she commented. Sometimes the two hippos would chase the beach ball all over the place, making Darlene giggle at their clumsy antics.

"Hey, anyone home?" Aaron called from the entrance to the nursery.

"I'm over here," Darlene replied, smiling as he approached her.

"Where's Ellen?" he asked, bending down to say hello to Skeeter, the chimp.

"She had to go out for a few minutes. Hang on—I'll be finished here in just a second." Darlene finished filling the pool, then shut off the water. Then she threw a mixture of fruit, vegetables, and grass into the hippos' pen and stepped out. "What are you doing over here so early this morning?" she asked Aaron, noticing as always how handsome he looked. He was wearing a royal-blue shirt that made his eyes look more blue than hazel, and his jeans were well worn, molding to his long legs.

"I'm going to be working here from now on," he replied with a big grin.

"*Here*, in the nursery?" Darlene exclaimed, feeling a little tingle of excitement at the thought of working side-by-side with Aaron every day. "How come?" she asked curiously. "What about the lions and tigers?"

"We're going to move Chelsea over here this morning," Aaron told her. He picked up a banana that was lying on the counter. "You know that caged area outside the back door?"

Darlene nodded, remembering the large cage that was nearly hidden by tall weeds and overgrown grass.

"We're putting Chelsea in there so she'll have more privacy when she gives birth," he explained as he peeled the banana and shoved it through the mesh top of Skeeter's playpen. "Doc Rockwell is relatively new at zoo medicine and he's never had a tigress give birth. He wants me to keep an eye on Chelsea, make notes on her behavior and stuff like that."

"Is Chelsea that close to having her cubs?" Darlene asked.

"Doc thinks it could be any time in the next week or two. A tigress only carries a baby for about three and a half months. Pretty different from humans," Aaron said.

Darlene was impressed. "I didn't know that." She looked at him with open admiration. "You know so much about animals."

Aaron shrugged. "That's because I love them. When all the other kids were outside playing, I was inside reading books about animals." He grinned at Darlene teasingly. "I also know something else. Last week after I took you to visit Chelsea, she told me she really likes you. She's glad she'll be here so you can visit her again."

"Oh, really, she told you that?" Darlene laughed. "Do the animals talk to you often?"

"Sure," Aaron said solemnly. "Just the other day Skeeter here told me he thought you were pretty cool." His eyes sparkled warmly. "He also told me that he thinks you're the prettiest girl working at the zoo."

Darlene felt a blush start down at her toes and spread all the way up to cover her face. "You're crazy," she murmured, both pleased and embarrassed by his words. "But it's a nice kind of crazy," she added shyly. For a long moment they smiled at each other in silence.

"Anyway, Chelsea's looking forward to seeing you again," Aaron said finally.

"I'm looking forward to it, too." Darlene grinned at him. "Be sure and tell her that, okay?"

He nodded, glancing over to the display

window. "Uh-oh—looks like you have visitors."

Darlene turned around and her eyes widened. There, on the other side of the glass, were her mom and dad, grinning broadly, and Kevin with his nose mashed against the window. All three of them were wearing the safari hats sold at the concession stands, their names stitched across the front of each one. They looked totally ridiculous, Darlene thought. As she stared at them, her parents waved and smiled broadly, and Kevin stuck out his tongue.

"Do you know those people?" Aaron asked curiously.

Darlene forced a smile. "That's my family," she replied, waving back. *Why, oh why do they have to look so silly, especially in front of Aaron? He'll never ask me out for a date if he thinks my family is a bunch of clowns,* she thought.

"Aren't you going to introduce me? They look like fun," Aaron said, much to her surprise.

"Well—sure," she answered, leading the way out of the nursery.

"Surprise!" Mr. Sullivan said with a smile. "I'll bet for a minute you thought I was Tarzan in my jungle hat." He scratched under his arm like a monkey and Kevin giggled and did the same thing.

"Oh, *please!*" Darlene groaned, mortified that they were acting so foolishly.

Kevin grinned at Darlene. "They made me promise not to tell you that we were coming to the zoo today," he said. "I can keep a secret real good." He looked enormously pleased with himself.

"Mom, Dad, this is a friend of mine, Aaron Caldwell." Darlene turned to Kevin. "Aaron works with the lions and tigers."

"Awesome!" Kevin looked at Aaron, impressed.

"That sounds dangerous," Darlene's mother said.

"It's really not," Aaron assured her. "The first thing we're taught is safety, and the zoo-keeper doesn't allow us to do anything that would put us in real danger."

"Well, that's a relief," Mrs. Sullivan said.

Darlene smiled at Aaron. "Mom is a champion worrier."

"Isn't that what mothers are for?" laughed Aaron.

"I wanna see the spider monkey," Kevin interrupted.

"That's him in the incubator." Darlene pointed to where the spider monkey lay sleeping. "If you wait just a few minutes, when I go back inside I'll lift him up to the window so you can get a closer look."

"Honey, we won't keep you any longer," Mr. Sullivan said. "We don't want to cause you any problems with your job. We just wanted to stop by and say hi."

"Besides, this is the first stop we made. We still have the rest of the zoo to see," Mrs. Sullivan added.

"Do you get to play with the lions?" Kevin asked, obviously still fascinated by Aaron's job.

"No, lions aren't really good to play with. But I do get to feed them," Aaron explained.

"Awesome! What do they eat?"

Aaron grinned. "Anything they want," he joked. "Actually, they eat big chunks of raw meat."

"Yuck!" Kevin made a face.

"I'd better get back inside," Darlene said. "Ellen's not here—she's my boss—and the animals aren't supposed to be left alone."

"Okay. Aaron, it was a pleasure meeting you," Mr. Sullivan said. He and Mrs. Sullivan shook Aaron's hand.

"Nice meeting you, too," Aaron answered. Then he and Darlene went back into the nursery. Darlene hurried over to the incubator and lifted out the tiny spider monkey, who grabbed hold of her smock like a baby holding on to its mother. She carried it to the window and held it up so Kevin could see. When he'd finished looking, all three Sullivans waved and walked away.

"Your family seems really nice," Aaron said as she put the spider monkey back in the incubator.

"Yeah, they're pretty cool," Darlene agreed. "But sometimes they're kind of silly—wearing those dopey hats. And I wanted to drop through the floor when Dad and Kevin started acting like monkeys!"

"Oh, I think that's neat. They were just having a good time," Aaron said. "It's nice when parents have a sense of humor."

"I guess you're right," Darlene said, pleased that he hadn't been turned off.

"Well, I'd better get back over to Chelsea," Aaron said. "She'll be pretty nervous when they start to move her and I want to be there to help calm her down. I just wanted to stop by and let you know that we're going to be coworkers." He smiled at Darlene, that teasing, flirtatious smile that made her toes curl up in her sneakers. "Personally, I'm glad. I can't think of anyone I'd rather work with."

"Me, too," Darlene answered breathlessly.

"I'll see you later, when we get Chelsea all settled in."

"Okay—see you." Darlene watched him leave, and at the same moment Ellen walked in.

"It looks like we're going to have another boarder," Ellen said. "I guess Aaron told you about Chelsea being moved over here, right?"

"Yes, he said she's going to have her cub pretty soon."

"Cubs," Ellen corrected. "Doc Rockwell thinks Chelsea may be carrying at least two and possibly even three cubs. Two is pretty common, but more than that is unusual. That's why he wants her isolated, so nothing will upset her."

"Aaron's really excited about being in charge of her," Darlene said.

Ellen grinned slyly. "And I bet you aren't too unhappy about him working here in the nursery." She laughed as Darlene blushed. "Aaron never spent much time over here until you came."

Darlene giggled, but her laughter died as she and Ellen heard the shouts of several men and the angry roar of a tiger coming from outside.

They both ran out to see four men pulling a wheeled cage toward the nursery. Inside the cage was an upset Chelsea. She paced back and forth, growling and snarling at the men who pulled the cage. Aaron was following closely, looking worried.

"You know the man in the white shirt, right?" Ellen asked Darlene.

Darlene nodded. "Ben Walkman, the head zookeeper. He hired me."

"Right. The man in the striped overalls is Walt Jacobs, the head keeper of the cats. The other two are assistant keepers."

The men pulled the cage around the back of the nursery to Chelsea's new home. They positioned the wheeled cage in front of the new cage door, then opened both doors, waiting for her to go from the small portable cage into the larger one. Darlene noticed that a slab of fresh meat had been placed in the new cage, but Chelsea didn't seem interested. She just kept pacing back and forth in the small wheeled cage, growling.

"She's really scared," Aaron said, coming over to stand next to Darlene and Ellen. "She's suspicious of the new cage and afraid to go into it." He stiffened and scowled as one of the assistant keepers picked up a long pole and attempted to prod the tigress into the new area. "I wish they wouldn't do that! If they'd just give her a little time, she'll eventually go in."

But the keeper kept gently prodding, and finally Chelsea stalked into her new cage, lashing her tail. The men quickly secured the door, then pulled the portable cage away.

"Darlene, let's go back inside. It's time to feed the babies," Ellen said, heading for the entrance to the nursery.

"I've got to go. I'll see you later." Darlene

smiled at Aaron and impulsively touched his arm. "Don't worry. I'm sure Chelsea is going to be just fine."

He forced a smile. "Thanks. I'm going to stay with her for a while—I'll be in later."

Shortly after twelve o'clock, Ellen told Darlene to take her lunch break. Darlene went out the back door and found Aaron sitting on the ground next to the cage, speaking softly to the restless tigress.

"It's okay, girl. You're going to be just fine," he murmured, trying to soothe Chelsea.

"Hi," Darlene said at last, coming up to stand beside Aaron. She kept her voice low and soft as she asked, "How's she doing?"

His eyes fixed on the tigress, Aaron replied, "Okay, but she's still really nervous. I'd like to stroke her, but I'm afraid she might bite me because she's upset."

"It's time for lunch," Darlene said.

Aaron shook his head. "I don't think I'll go to lunch today. I'd rather stay here with Chelsea." He smiled at Darlene shyly. "I guess it sounds crazy, but I think she likes me being here with her."

"It doesn't sound crazy at all," Darlene protested. Then she had an idea. "Why don't I go to get us each a hot dog and a soda and come back here to sit with you?" she asked tentatively. "I could keep you and Chelsea company—that is, if you think she wouldn't mind."

Aaron smiled at her warmly. "I'm sure she wouldn't. And I know I'd like that. I'll be eating lunch with my two favorite girls!"

Chapter Seven

"So, what's the deal with you and Aaron?" Chrissy asked Darlene at the concession hut a week later.

"What do you mean?" Darlene asked innocently, squirting more mustard on her hot dog.

"She means that you and Aaron seem to be getting awfully chummy," Amy said. "You eat lunch with him more than you do with us."

"There's nothing going on," Darlene protested.

"Then why are you always with him?" Amy asked, taking one of Darlene's potato chips.

As casually as she could, Darlene said, "Since they moved Chelsea into the nursery, Aaron has been working there with me. It's only natural that as coworkers, we're spending a lot of time together."

"*Working* with him? Is that what makes your face turn red every time his name is mentioned?" Chrissy giggled again as Darlene blushed.

"Oh, lay off, you guys," Alysia said. "You're all just jealous because it's obvious Aaron likes Darlene."

"How many dates have you had with him?" Kate asked, eyeing Darlene closely.

"None," Darlene admitted.

"*None?*" Amy and Kate shouted in surprise.

"I thought maybe you'd managed to do what none of us could—get more than one or two dates with Aaron Caldwell," Chrissy added.

Darlene shook her head. "I told you, we're just coworkers. He hasn't asked me out even once."

"Maybe he does like you, but maybe he likes you as a friend, not a girlfriend," Kate suggested. "I mean, Aaron's not exactly shy.

If he wanted to ask you out, he would have by now."

For the rest of the day, Darlene was haunted by Kate's words. Though she had told herself originally that all she wanted was Aaron's friendship, everything was different now that she'd fallen in love with him. There was nothing worse than being in love with a guy who only wanted to be friends!

As she fed the bear cub, she thought about the previous Saturday. She'd met Aaron at the swimming pool, and he'd kept his promise, teaching her how to dog-paddle and float on her back. He'd been wonderfully patient with her, and they had laughed so hard that Darlene's sides had ached.

Darlene looked up to see the object of her thoughts coming through the back door to the nursery. "Hi," she said brightly, glad that thoughts couldn't be read on people's faces.

"I've been thinking . . ." he began.

Darlene grinned. "Was it a new experience for you?" she teased, laughing as he pretended to scowl at her.

"Actually, I was thinking about you," he continued. "I'll bet you haven't had a chance to enjoy the zoo like a guest this summer."

"You're right," Darlene agreed. "I've been so busy working here, this is the first summer I haven't had time just to visit like a normal person."

"Why don't we hang out after work tonight for a couple of hours and pretend we don't work here?" Aaron suggested. "The zoo doesn't close until seven."

Excited at the prospect of spending a couple of hours with him, Darlene agreed. While this wasn't really an official date, it was a beginning!

At exactly five o'clock that evening, Aaron and Darlene left the nursery together.

"If we're going to see the zoo like 'normal' people, there's something we have to do first," he said, heading for a concession stand.

"Oh, no!" Darlene laughed as he pointed out the silly safari hats like the ones her family had worn.

"Oh, yes," Aaron replied and instructed the girl working there to stitch his name on one and Darlene's on another. "There!" he said, grinning as he put on his hat, then placed hers on her head. "Now we look like a couple of tourists." He grabbed hold of Darlene's hand. "What do you want to see first?"

"Oh, I don't know—the polar bears! No, the monkeys—or maybe the reptile house . . ." Darlene began.

"I can tell I'm going to have to make all the decisions in this relationship," Aaron joked.

Darlene's heart lurched in her chest. A relationship—was that what they had? She definitely liked the sound of it. Smiling at Aaron, she said, "Okay. So what are we going to see first?"

"We're going to see my favorite animal after the cats," Aaron told her.

"The elephants?" Darlene guessed.

"Nope," he said, releasing her hand and putting his arm around her shoulders. "Guess again."

"Uh—the zebras?" she murmured. She was having trouble thinking straight with Aaron so close to her. A boy didn't put his arm around a girl's shoulders like that if he only thought of her as a friend, did he? How could she think about animals when her head was so filled with thoughts of Aaron?

"Wrong again." He looked down at her, his sunny smile warming her from the outside in. "The giraffes. They're my second favorite animal."

"Oh, terrific! I like them, too." She would have said the same thing if he'd said that about any animal.

"Giraffes are so unusual-looking," Darlene said, as they watched the tall creatures munching on the leaves of the surrounding trees. "And they're so graceful, too."

"Did you know that giraffes can close their nostrils completely to keep out dust and sand?" Aaron asked.

Darlene giggled. "That's a trick I'd like to learn for my swimming lessons!"

"You don't have to worry about getting water up your nose unless you put your head underwater." He grinned at her. "Last Saturday you didn't get one strand of hair wet."

"I will one of these days," she laughed. "Maybe next summer!"

Aaron sobered slightly, looking again at the giraffes. "This African display is my favorite because all the animals are in a habitat like their natural one." He gestured at the wide expanse of grass and trees. "At least here the animals have plenty of room to roam." He frowned. "It's too bad so many of the others are cooped up in cages. It's cruel to the animals. There are a lot of animal rights groups that are really upset about it, including one right here in Glendale."

Darlene nodded absently, not wanting to talk about something so serious. She didn't want to have to think about anything at the moment, except how wonderful it was to be with Aaron.

Aaron grinned at her, then he steered her toward the polar bears. After they watched the huge, yellowish-white animals playing in their pools of cold water, they paid a visit to the elk and deer in a large fenced enclosure. The sea lions' funny antics made them laugh, and as they wandered along, Aaron entertained Darlene with facts about the animals they saw and told her stories about his three summers working at the zoo.

When they got tired of walking, they rode the little train that took visitors all over the park. Just before they left, Aaron bought Darlene a figurine of a tiger for a souvenir and she knew she would cherish it for the rest of her life.

"That was so much fun!" Darlene sighed as they walked hand-in-hand to her car.

"It was the best time I've ever had visiting the zoo," Aaron said.

Darlene smiled. "It's always nice doing something like this with a friend."

Aaron leaned close to her. "I don't think of you as a friend, Darlene," he said softly. "You mean a lot more to me than that."

Darlene was so thrilled that she couldn't speak. Her heart was beating so loudly and so fast she was sure he could hear it.

"Well, you'd better get out of here or your folks will wonder what happened to you," he said, opening her car door for her.

"Thanks," Darlene managed to say, holding her tiger tightly in her hand. "Can I give you a lift?"

He shook his head. "My car's around the corner. See you tomorrow morning." He closed the door after she had gotten in, then waved and stepped up onto the curb.

"Come down from there!" Darlene said sternly to Skeeter three days later. The little chimp had once again escaped from his play-pen and was sitting on top of the refrigerator, but this time it didn't bother Darlene that he was loose. Skeeter had gotten out at least a dozen times since she had first started working in the nursery, and she knew it would be only a matter of time before she could coax him back into his pen.

Skeeter bared his teeth at her and shook his head, as if he knew exactly what she was saying. Darlene laughed. Of all the animals she had helped care for in the nursery, Skeeter had become her favorite. Maybe it was because he had been largely responsible for her meeting Aaron. Or maybe it was just because he was so cute and so ridiculously stubborn!

"Come on, Skeeter. We don't have time for your nonsense this morning," Ellen said. "We're getting a baby gorilla later this afternoon. I've got to get a cage cleaned and ready for the new arrival."

"You talk to him like he can really understand you," Darlene said, laughing.

"Sometimes I think he can." Ellen laughed, too. "He's just like a mischievous little kid. But the little stinker is going back to Monkey Island today. As soon as we catch him, I'm supposed to take him over."

"You mean Skeeter's leaving the nursery?" Darlene felt a lump forming in her throat.

"They all do sooner or later," Ellen said cheerfully. "Come on, Skeeter. Stop fooling around."

Skeeter jumped down into Darlene's arms and buried his head in her shoulder. Darlene patted his furry little head, feeling ridiculously close to tears at the thought of the nursery without Skeeter's silly escapades. She hadn't realized how attached she'd gotten to him until this very moment.

"Let's go, Skeeter. It's time for you to go back where you belong," Ellen said, trying to take the monkey from Darlene.

But Skeeter clung even more tightly. "He doesn't want to go," Darlene said around the lump in her throat.

"Well, he has to," Ellen said briskly. "Besides, he doesn't really know what's going on. He's just being his usual stubborn self." She finally managed to pry the monkey's arms from around Darlene's neck. "I'll be back in a little while. I'm going to take him over to Monkey Island."

Darlene nodded sadly, unable to speak because she was afraid she was going to cry.

"Good morning," Aaron said as he came into the nursery.

"Morning," Darlene mumbled, turning away and wiping at her tears with the back of her hand.

"Hey, what's wrong?" He put his hands on her shoulders and turned her around to face him. "You're crying."

"I'm so dumb . . ." Darlene forced a little laugh, blinking back more tears.

"You are not dumb," Aaron protested. "Tell me why you're crying. Did Ellen yell at you or something?"

She shook her head, feeling ridiculous. She pointed to the empty playpen. "Ellen just took Skeeter back to Monkey Island." She tried to control her quivering lips, hoping she wouldn't start crying again.

"Oh." Aaron immediately understood. "That's why you're sad. It's always hard to say good-bye to an animal when it leaves here." He pulled her into his arms to comfort her. Darlene rested her head on his shoulder the way Skeeter had done when she had held him. She felt so safe and secure in Aaron's arms.

"I just didn't realize I'd gotten so attached to him. He always made me laugh." She hid her face in Aaron's shirt, feeling the tears still burning her eyes. "Sometimes, when I'd given him a banana, he'd break it in half and give part of it to me, like he wanted to share with me." She choked on a little sob. "I'm really going to miss him."

"I know," he murmured, smoothing her hair with his hand. "But it's important that he get back to Monkey Island where he can be with other monkeys and live as normal a life as he can, considering he'll still be in captivity. He'd never be completely happy shut up in here."

Darlene knew Aaron was right. Skeeter belonged with others of his own kind, not in a pen in the nursery. "I didn't really think about it that way, I guess," she admitted.

Aaron smiled down at her. "I think that's what I like best about you. You think with your heart and not with your head." And then, before Darlene realized what he was going to do, he kissed her. His lips were warm and soft on hers, making her breath stick in her throat. One minute he was kissing her, and the next minute he was smiling at her as though nothing unusual had happened. "We'll go visit Skeeter at Monkey

Island," he promised. "Now, I guess this is a good time to ask you a question."

"What?" Darlene asked breathlessly, still dazed by his kiss.

"There's a movie playing at the Triplex that I'd really like to see. Would you like to go with me this Friday night?"

Darlene stepped back a little, looking at him in delighted astonishment. "You mean, like a date? A real date?"

"That's what I had in mind," he laughed. "So what do you say? Will you go?"

"Yes!" she answered without hesitation. "Yes, yes, yes!"

Chapter Eight

"You've been running around the house like a chicken without a head. Is there something special about this date tonight?" Mr. Sullivan asked on Friday evening.

"It's only the most important date of my entire life!" Darlene answered. She was so nervous that she was beginning to wonder if she'd be able to get through the night without throwing up. Wouldn't *that* be the perfect way to ruin her first date with Aaron! She hurried back to her room to finish getting ready. Aaron was due to arrive in fifteen minutes and she still had to brush her hair and finish putting on her makeup.

Never in Darlene's dating experience had she been so nervous, never had she been so completely crazy about a guy.

Please, please don't let anything terrible happen, she pleaded silently as she ran a brush through her hair. *Please don't let me do anything stupid to mess things up!*

Darlene finished styling her hair, displeased with it as usual, but decided it was as good as it was going to get. At least she had a brand-new outfit to wear. The short blue-denim skirt hugged her hips, and with the pale-pink sleeveless blouse tucked in, she knew she looked pretty. She had just finished her makeup when her father called, "Darlene, honey, your young man is here."

Darlene groaned under her breath at her dad's words. "Okay, I'll be right out," she called. She gave her hair one final flick with the brush, then sprayed her favorite cologne over her neck and shoulders. Finally, taking a deep breath and crossing her fingers in hopes that nothing would go wrong, she went out into the living room.

Aaron was there with her family, looking more handsome than she'd ever seen him. He was wearing white pants and a mint-green shirt that made his hazel eyes glow with green flecks. He stood up from the sofa as she entered the room.

"Hi," he said, smiling, and she could tell by the way he looked at her that he liked what he saw.

"Aaron was just telling us all about Chelsea," Mrs. Sullivan said to Darlene. "It must be very exciting, anticipating the birth of tiger cubs."

"It's a wonderful opportunity," Darlene's father added. "Very few people get to see something like that."

Aaron nodded. "The zoo has somebody watching Chelsea twenty-four hours a day. I made sure that whoever is on duty will call me when she goes into labor." He glanced over at Darlene. "And as soon as they call, I'm going to call Darlene. That way, maybe we can get there in time for the birth."

"Shouldn't we be on our way?" Darlene suggested to Aaron. She loved her family, but she didn't want to spend the whole evening with them. And she had a feeling that if her parents and Kevin started talking animals with Aaron, they'd never get to the movies.

"Sure," Aaron agreed. "It was nice seeing

you again," he said to her parents. "Kevin, I've got a great book about tigers at home. I'll bring it to work on Monday and Darlene can bring it home for you to look at."

"Awesome!" Kevin answered in his usual fashion.

"Drive carefully, Aaron. And don't forget your curfew, Darlene," Mrs. Sullivan called after them.

"I've never been late for curfew, but she says that every time I go out," Darlene told Aaron as they walked toward his car.

Aaron laughed good-naturedly. "That's just more of the stuff moms are supposed to say. Every morning before I leave for work my mom asks me if I have lunch money. I've never forgotten money for lunch since I was eight years old, but she still says it every day." He opened the car door for her. "I think mothers say things like that because they don't want us to grow up." He closed the door, then went around to the driver's side. Darlene buckled her seat belt and he buckled his.

"That was nice of you, to offer to bring the book for Kevin," she said as Aaron started the engine.

He shrugged his shoulders. "It's no big deal."

"So, what's this movie we're going to see? You never did tell me," she said once he had started the car and pulled away from the curb.

"Actually, it's sort of a documentary. I didn't want to tell you because I thought you might not want to go," he explained. Darlene smiled, thinking she would watch a blank screen for hours if it meant spending time with him. "Anyway, it's on wildlife at the North Pole."

"That sounds really interesting," she said. "You know how much I love animals."

Darlene looked down at Aaron's hands on the steering wheel. He had long, slender fingers. She knew how warm and strong his hands felt when they were holding hers, and she imagined they would also feel good to a wounded or frightened animal. She was sure Aaron would be a fine vet some day.

"Are you going to meet me tomorrow at the pool again?" he asked. "I'm determined to get you swimming by the end of the summer."

"Sure," Darlene replied. "Although I don't know if there's enough summer left for me to learn to actually swim." She didn't want to think about the end of summer. When summer was over, her job at the zoo would be over. And she and Aaron would be going to different high schools. She wouldn't be able to see him every day, and that thought made her unhappy.

"I can tell what you're thinking by the expression on your face," Aaron said, giving her a quick glance, then looking back at the road. "You're thinking that summer's half over. I always hate the thought of it, too, but I think I hate it more this summer than ever before." He took one hand off the steering wheel and reached over to take Darlene's hand. "This has been one of the best summers I've ever had, and it's mostly because of you."

For a moment, Darlene couldn't speak. Her heart seemed to swell and fill her whole chest, making it difficult for her to speak. "I feel the same way about you," she finally managed to choke out.

"But the summer isn't over *yet*," Aaron pointed out. "We'll just have to make the most of the time we do have."

Darlene nodded, happier than she'd ever been in her life.

"Now, let me ask you a really important question," Aaron said, releasing her hand so he could pull into the movie theater parking lot. He parked the car, then turned and looked at her seriously. After a long pause, he asked, "Do you like your popcorn buttered or unbuttered?"

"Definitely buttered," Darlene answered with a giggle.

"Whew!" He breathed an exaggerated sigh of relief. "For a minute there I thought we were going to have to call this whole date off. I can't possibly go to the movies with a girl who doesn't like buttered popcorn."

"You're in luck," Darlene laughed. "Butter's my middle name!"

"Good." He grinned and together they got out of the car and headed for the theater entrance. As soon as Aaron had bought their tickets, he took Darlene to the concession stand and bought the biggest tub of buttered popcorn they sold, along with two sodas.

"We'll *never* eat all this," Darlene protested

as they found seats near the front of the theater.

"Yes, we will. You watch—before the movie's over, we'll be fighting each other for the drippy kernels left at the bottom."

Though Darlene wasn't much into documentaries, the minute the film began she became engrossed in the real-life drama unfolding on the screen. But she wasn't so absorbed that she was unaware of Aaron's presence next to her, especially when he put his arm around her shoulders and pulled her close.

So far, everything was going wonderfully. She hadn't spilled her soda or knocked the popcorn onto the floor. And she hadn't said or done anything really dumb. Darlene hoped that Aaron would ask her out again and again. She shivered at the thought and Aaron tightened his arm around her.

Darlene looked at Aaron for a long moment, unable to believe that he seemed to like her every bit as much as she liked him. The warnings of the other girls seemed like nothing but sour grapes. Sure, maybe Aaron had only gone out with Kate, Amy, and Chrissy once or twice, but she couldn't believe he wouldn't want to keep dating her after tonight. She and Aaron were so right for each other. They both loved the zoo, they both wanted eventually to become veterinarians, and they even enjoyed the same type of food.

When the movie finally ended, Darlene was very much aware that each minute that passed brought her closer to her curfew and the end of her date with Aaron.

"How about some tacos?" he asked as they left the theater. "I know a little Mexican restaurant not too far from here." He looked at his wristwatch. "We've got plenty of time before you have to get home."

"I couldn't eat a bite," Darlene replied, stuffed from all the popcorn she'd eaten. "But I could sit and watch *you* eat."

A few minutes later, they were seated at a table in the back of the Mexican Hat Restaurant.

"How did you ever find this place?" Darlene asked after the waitress had taken their order and headed for the kitchen. "I've been by here at least a hundred times, but I never even realized it was a restaurant."

"They don't do much advertising," Aaron

said. "But my dad knows every Mexican restaurant for miles around. He's a real burrito freak. Once we drove two hours to a restaurant where he heard they served the best burritos north of the border."

"And were they the best?" Darlene asked curiously.

"Nah, at least Dad didn't think so. He's still on his quest to find the perfect burrito."

Darlene laughed. "He sounds like fun."

"He is," Aaron agreed. "Maybe next time we go out, we'll stop by my house so you can meet him and my mom."

"I'd like that," she said, feeling so happy she thought she might burst. *Next time . . .* it was almost as good as a promise that he was going to ask her out again!

The waitress brought their sodas, then placed a platter of six huge tacos in front of Aaron.

As he ate, they talked about other movies they had seen and other restaurants they'd been to. Aaron coaxed Darlene into taking a bite of his taco, and she agreed that it was the best she'd ever tasted, although she secretly thought what made it taste so wonderful was the fact that she was sharing it with Aaron.

When Aaron had finished eating and paid the bill, they left the restaurant, walking slowly, hand-in-hand, toward his car.

"Look at all the stars!" Darlene tilted her head back to look up in awe. The entire night sky was glittering with brilliant stars, and she had the feeling they were shining especially for her and Aaron.

"They are pretty, aren't they?" he agreed. They stopped at the passenger side of his car, but instead of opening the door, Aaron drew her into his arms. "I've been wanting to do this all night," he said huskily, and then he kissed her.

It wasn't like the first time they'd kissed, over almost before Darlene knew what was happening. This time his mouth lingered on hers, his lips warm, stealing the very breath out of her body. And Darlene knew absolutely, positively that she was head over heels in love with Aaron Caldwell.

Chapter Nine

"Doc Rockwell said I can name the tiger cubs when they're born," Aaron said as they got into the car.

Still a little light-headed and dizzy from his kiss, Darlene said, "That's great. Have you thought of any good names?"

"Not yet. I was sort of hoping you might help me think of some."

Darlene laughed. "Oh, I'm terrible at naming animals! I let Kevin name any new pets we get because I always come up with something dumb."

Aaron took her hand and smiled at her. "I can't imagine you doing anything dumb."

"You'd be surprised," she said with a grin

as he let go of her hand and started the car. "Hey, I have an idea! If it's twins, you could name them what Alysia calls her twin sisters—Rude and Crude."

Aaron laughed. "Actually, I was thinking of something a little more noble-sounding." He looked at his wristwatch. "It looks like I'm going to get you home before your curfew."

"That will make my parents happy," Darlene said, smiling at him.

"Good. I want to keep them happy with me," Aaron said, returning her smile. "That way maybe they won't mind if I want to take you out every night of the week."

I've definitely died and gone to heaven, Darlene thought.

"Have you heard the rumor going around?" he asked.

"No, what rumor?" Darlene asked dreamily. She didn't really care about rumors. She didn't care about anything except the fact that Aaron had kissed her and wanted to date her again. The evening had been totally perfect and her life couldn't be more wonderful than it was right this very moment.

"I've heard that the zoo might close down," Aaron answered.

His words brought Darlene out of her dreamy state and she stared at him in astonishment. "*What?* You're kidding, right?"

"No. It's true, and personally I hope it *does* close down," Aaron said, pulling into the Sullivans' driveway and shutting off the car engine.

"What do you mean?" Darlene asked incredulously. "How can you even say that?" She stared at Aaron as if she'd never seen him before. Was this the same guy who was so crazy about Chelsea? Was this the same guy who had worked at the zoo for the past three summers? "Aaron, I don't understand," she said. "You work at the zoo. Why would you want to see it close?"

Aaron didn't say anything for a moment. He just sat there frowning, as if he was trying to find the right words. "You know how much I love animals," he began at last. "The zoo is the only place around where I can work with the kinds of animals I want to. But lately I've been thinking that zoos are wrong. I think they shouldn't exist at all."

"I can't believe you're saying that!" Darlene was stunned. "I *love* the zoo! Some of my happiest memories are of visiting the zoo with my family. Going to the zoo is a tradition for lots of families." She unbuckled her seat belt and turned around to face Aaron. "If kids couldn't go to a zoo, how would they ever get to see real live elephants, and tigers, and other exotic wild animals from faraway places?"

"They can read about them in books, or watch documentaries on television," Aaron replied. He was still frowning, and his eyes were no longer warm, but filled with frustration and disappointment. "You know, Darlene, I thought you and I had so much in common. I guess I was wrong. How can you think it's okay to put wild animals behind bars as if they were criminals or something? You've seen the way a lot of them pace back and forth, miserable because they can't run free through a jungle or on the plains like they're supposed to. How would you like it if somebody put *you* in a cage?"

"I wouldn't like it one bit. But I'm a human and those are animals. And how can they miss what they've never had? Lots of the zoo animals were born in captivity. They don't know any other life."

"Oh, so that makes it all right?" Aaron said sarcastically. "Being cooped up in cages is unhealthy not only physically but mentally for most animals. That's why they grow listless and sluggish, and it's why a lot of species don't breed in captivity."

Darlene had never seen him look so angry. "I'll agree that there are some problems with the zoo system, but the answer isn't to just close all the zoos," she protested hotly.

"People like you make me so mad," Aaron continued, as if he hadn't heard her. "You're willing to sacrifice the lives and comfort of animals just so you can go to stare at them in a zoo and eat hot dogs and wear funny hats. You don't really care about how the animals feel!"

"How dare you say that!" Darlene cried, anger racing through her. It was one thing for him to disagree with her about the importance of zoos, but it was quite another for him to accuse her of not caring about animals. "I love animals as much as you do," she retorted heatedly. "But I also think zoos are good. They're educational as well as entertaining, and a lot of the animals are better off there than they would be in the wild."

She glared at Aaron. "You have no right to say I don't care about the animals!"

Aaron ran his fingers through his hair, obviously as angry as she was. "I've volunteered to work with the animal rights group that wants to close down the zoo. This is a subject that's really important to me, and I was hoping it would be important to you, too. I was hoping maybe you'd work on it with me."

Darlene shook her head vehemently. The sick feeling that had started in the pit of her stomach was spreading throughout her whole body. "No way! I couldn't possibly work with a group like that because I *do* believe in zoos, and I *don't* want the Glendale Zoo torn down!"

They were both silent for a long moment. The only sounds were the chirping of crickets in the Sullivans' yard and the distant barking of a dog. "I guess that does it, then," Aaron said with a finality that made Darlene's heart drop down to her feet.

"Yeah, I guess that does it," she whispered. She opened the car door, feeling tears of anger and frustration burning in her eyes. "You don't have to walk me to the door.

Thanks for the movie." Before Aaron could say anything else, Darlene jumped out of the car and ran to her front door. She hurried into the house, shut the door behind her and leaned against it. The tears she'd been holding back flowed freely down her cheeks. She'd blown it. This time she'd blown it for sure.

Darlene wiped away the tears with the back of her hand, glad her parents were in bed so she didn't have to answer any questions. Feeling miserable, she went into her bedroom, changed into her nightgown, and crawled into bed.

Why hadn't she just kept her big mouth shut? Why hadn't she just agreed with everything Aaron had said? If she had, they wouldn't have fought and then the date would have ended happily. She should have said she'd join the animal rights group, too.

Yet Darlene realized that she could never have done that. She couldn't set aside her personal beliefs just to please a guy, no matter how important the guy was to her. But any way she looked at it, the truth was clear: she was in love with Aaron, and that was what hurt the most.

Darlene turned over on her side, her gaze focusing on the tiger figurine Aaron had bought for her the evening they had visited the zoo. The moonlight streamed in her bedroom window and shone on the tiger, making its striped golden coat glisten. Why hadn't he told her how he felt about zoos then? Why hadn't he told her the first day she'd met him, or when they had gone to the swimming pool, or any of the times they'd eaten lunch together? Why hadn't he told her before she'd fallen hopelessly in love with him?

Chapter Ten

Darlene and Alysia walked across the zoo parking lot together on Monday morning. "I tried to call you all day yesterday, but your mom said you weren't feeling well. Is that why you didn't go to the pool on Saturday?"

"That was one of the reasons," Darlene replied. Even though she and Aaron had an agreement to meet at the pool every Saturday, she'd figured that after their argument Friday night, he wouldn't want to help her learn to swim anymore. But she couldn't help asking, "Was Aaron there?"

"No. I sort of figured maybe the two of you had decided to do something else together,"

Alysia said. Then she grinned and looked at Darlene expectantly. "So?"

"So what?" Darlene asked, although she knew exactly what Alysia wanted to know.

Alysia rolled her dark eyes. "Tell me about your date Friday night! What did you do? Where did you go?"

"We went to the movies, then to a Mexican restaurant," Darlene answered, dreading the questions she was sure Alysia was going to ask next.

Alysia stopped in her tracks. "Darlene Sullivan, I thought we were getting to be close friends!"

"We are." Darlene stopped too and avoided Alysia's eyes.

"Then why are you making it so obvious that you don't want to tell me about your date with Aaron?" Alysia demanded.

"Because I messed everything up and I don't want to talk about it," Darlene muttered.

"What do you mean, you messed everything up?" Alysia waved to Gus, then hurried through the gate to catch up with Darlene. "*How* did you mess everything up?"

"I disagreed with him about something

and we had a fight," Darlene explained miserably.

"About what?" Alysia asked, staring at her in surprise. "I thought you and Aaron got along so well. What could you possibly find to fight about?"

After a long pause, Darlene said, "Zoos."

"*Zoos?*" Alysia's forehead crinkled in confusion. "I don't understand."

"Did you know there's an animal rights group that wants to close the zoo?" Darlene asked.

"Yeah, I've heard something about it. My boss told me they want to tear this one down and build a more modern zoo, with the animals in more natural habitats. But a girl I work with said she heard they just want to tear it down and not rebuild at all." Alysia's frown deepened. "But what does that have to do with you and Aaron?"

Darlene sighed. "Friday night he asked me to join this animal rights group. He doesn't approve of keeping animals in cages. I told him I didn't want to see the zoo torn down. He got angry and we argued, and now we're through."

"Okay, so you guys don't agree on this particular topic. What's the big deal?" Alysia asked impatiently.

"It's very important to Aaron," Darlene told her.

"Look, I've got to go," Alysia said, glancing at her wristwatch. "I'm sure you and Aaron can work this out. I'll talk to you about it at lunch."

"Okay," Darlene replied, forcing a smile. She turned and headed down the path to the nursery building. For the first time since she had begun the job, she actually dreaded going to work today. She knew how much it was going to hurt to have to see Aaron, work with him, and know he didn't care about her anymore. It was going to be awful to see his eyes become indifferent and his smile turn cold when he looked at her. But she forced her feet to move toward the nursery, knowing she couldn't put it off any longer.

Darlene breathed a sigh of relief when she came into the nursery and found only Ellen there. "Oh, I'm so glad you're here," Ellen said. "Doc Rockwell is bringing in a baby kangaroo who got his foot stuck in some broken fencing. The infirmary is pretty full, so he wants us to keep the kangaroo in here for a while." She picked up her purse and took off her smock. "But I've got to run an errand, so you'll have to handle it, Darlene. Just put the kangaroo in the empty cage."

Darlene nodded, and Ellen left. As Darlene accomplished her morning tasks of preparing formula and feeding the animals, she thought of Alysia's words: "I'm sure you and Aaron can work this out," she had said.

Can we? Darlene wondered. They weren't the first couple to have differences of opinions on various topics. Couldn't she and Aaron agree to disagree when it came to the importance of zoos? She felt a faint flicker of hope, but her thoughts were interrupted by the arrival of Doc Rockwell.

"Hi, Doc," she greeted him, her gaze immediately going to the bundle he held in his arms.

"Hi, Darlene. I've got a new boarder for you." He turned down a corner of the blanket to expose the sleeping kangaroo, its foot wrapped in a huge bandage. "He'll probably sleep for a little while. I had to anesthetize him to do emergency surgery—he nearly severed his foot trying to escape."

Darlene took the little kangaroo from the

doctor's arms and gently laid him in the cage that Ellen had prepared for him. "Is he going to be all right?" she asked as the little fellow whimpered and curled up.

"He'll be fine," Doc Rockwell assured her. "Right now he just needs to sleep and let his body begin the healing process." He patted Darlene on the shoulder. "And now I'd better get back to work."

When he was gone, Darlene pulled a stool up beside the kangaroo's cage and sat down. *Poor little thing*, she thought, gazing at the brown furry animal. This was the sort of thing Aaron had been talking about, animals hurting themselves trying to escape from the confines of cages and fenced areas. Darlene was willing to admit that there were drawbacks to zoos, but surely the answer wasn't to close them all down.

Darlene sighed. She certainly didn't have any answers. All she knew was that her argument with Aaron didn't seem like a good enough reason for them not to date anymore. If only she could convince him of that!

She didn't have an opportunity to talk to Aaron that morning, because he didn't come into the nursery. But her hopes began to rise. The more she thought about it, the more ridiculous it seemed for them to allow a difference of opinion to ruin their relationship. Surely what they felt for each other was stronger than that.

At noon, when Ellen told her to go to lunch, Darlene finally got up the nerve to ask if Aaron had called in sick or something. Ellen told her that he'd been helping out over at the cat display all morning and was now probably at lunch. So when Darlene left the nursery and headed for the concession stand, her eyes darted around, looking for him.

As she rounded the corner of the concession hut, Darlene nearly bumped right into Aaron. He was standing with his back to her, talking to Ben Walkman, the head zookeeper. She backed around the corner again and decided to wait until his conversation was finished.

"She shouldn't be working in the nursery." Aaron's words drifted to where Darlene stood, making her breath catch in her throat. "She doesn't care about the animals, not really," he continued. That was exactly what he'd said to her Friday night, and now he was saying the same thing to the head zookeeper.

Darlene turned and ran in the other direction, her thoughts racing. What was he trying to do? Get her fired?

She came to a bench and sat down, still stunned by what she had overheard. What he'd done was unforgivable! He knew how much she loved working here. She knew now that she and Aaron would never get back together. Darlene wished she had stuck to her original rule: no more dating!

Chapter Eleven

Two hours later, Aaron walked into the nursery, and despite her anger at what he'd done, Darlene felt her heart flip-flop in her chest.

"Hi," she said coolly, while washing baby bottles and placing them in the sterilizer. Aaron moved closer to her. His fresh, clean scent surrounded her, making her close her eyes for a moment. It would be so much easier if she never had to see him again!

"So, what are you doing?" he asked casually.

She couldn't believe he was acting so nonchalant. Just a short while ago he was trying to get her fired, and now he was acting as if nothing were wrong.

"What does it look like I'm doing?" she answered.

"Darlene, we need to talk." He placed his hand gently on her shoulder.

She turned to face him and brushed his hand away. "What do we have to talk about?"

"We need to discuss what happened Friday night," he said, his eyes gazing earnestly into hers.

Darlene turned back around with a shrug and continued washing bottles. "There's nothing to talk about. We went out together, and we discovered we weren't right for each other. It was no big deal."

"Yes, it was," he insisted. "Would you stop working and talk to me?" he asked, his voice filled with frustration.

Taking a deep breath, Darlene once again turned around and faced him. "I'm listening," she said grimly.

Aaron sighed. "Look, I acted like a real jerk Friday night and I apologize," he began. He shoved his hands in his jeans pockets. "Everything was going so great and then I ruined it all by being so opinionated. I guess

I always get too excited when I start on the subject of zoos." He looked down at his feet for a moment, then back at her. "I guess I hoped you'd think just like me. I wanted you to believe what I believe. Anyway, I spent the whole weekend thinking about it, and—well, I don't care if we don't think alike. It's not important." He looked at her, his hazel eyes pleading. "Couldn't we just start over? Go out again?" He smiled at her tentatively. "And this time I'll know better than to talk about whether zoos are right or wrong."

Darlene was tempted to throw her arms around him. It would be so easy to forget the fight they'd had. But there was just one small problem. She couldn't forget his conversation with the zookeeper.

"Is there anything else you want to tell me?" she asked.

He looked at her, his brow wrinkled. "No, I just wanted you to know that it doesn't matter to me if you feel differently about zoos. I'd still like to go out with you."

Darlene's hopes died. There might have been a chance for them if he'd explained about what he'd said to the zookeeper, but he hadn't. "Look, Aaron," she said, "I had a good time Friday night, but I spent the weekend thinking too, and I've decided it's better if we don't go out again."

He looked surprised and hurt. "But I thought . . ." He broke off, running his hand through his hair and looking down at the floor. "Well, if that's the way you want it . . ."

"That's the way it has to be," she replied dully, wondering if it were possible to die of a broken heart.

"Darlene, honey," Mrs. Sullivan shook Darlene's shoulder gently.

Darlene rubbed her eyes and sat up, wondering why her mother was waking her up in the middle of the night. She looked at the clock on the bedside stand, surprised to see that it was only a few minutes after nine o'clock. She'd gone to bed right after supper, depressed.

"Aaron's on the phone," Mrs. Sullivan told Darlene. "He says that tigress is about to have her cubs and he wants to know if you'd like to ride with him over to the zoo. I told him you were sleeping, but he seemed sure you'd want to go." She frowned slightly. "Do you really think it's a good idea for you to go out, since you're so tired?"

"I really want to be there, Mom. We've been waiting all month for Chelsea to give birth, and I don't want to miss it." Darlene looked at her mother pleadingly. "Please Mom, let me go."

"All right. I'll tell him to come by for you."

As Mrs. Sullivan left the room, Darlene jumped out of bed and began dressing as fast as she could, thinking about the past week. It had been the most miserable week of her life. She and Aaron couldn't avoid each other, since they both worked in the nursery. And they had been overly polite to each other, talking only about their work. Darlene couldn't forgive Aaron, but she couldn't stop caring about him, either, even though every day she'd expected to be called down to the office and told that she was fired. Darlene couldn't stand the thought of losing the job she loved so much when she'd done nothing wrong.

Once dressed, she went into the living room where her parents were watching television. "I don't know how long I'll be," she told them.

"If nothing has happened by midnight, call

119

your father and me and one of us will pick you up," Mrs. Sullivan instructed.

"I promise," Darlene said. She went over and kissed her mother's cheek, grateful that her parents had allowed her to go out at all. Then she went into the hall and peered out the front door.

When Darlene saw the headlights of Aaron's car, she took a deep breath, knowing it was not going to be easy to be with him. Then she ran outside.

"Doc Rockwell says this is it," Aaron said as she got into the car. "I figured you wouldn't want to miss it in spite of—well, everything."

"Thanks," Darlene answered.

They didn't speak again. As he drove, Darlene kept sneaking glances at him out of the corner of her eye. Why did he have to be so handsome? Would her heart ever stop hammering whenever he was around? His hair was tousled by the breeze blowing in the open windows of the car, and Darlene stifled the impulse to lean over and smooth it down with her fingers.

They passed through the security gate, where a night watchman checked their badges, then they raced to Chelsea's cage. They found Doc Rockwell and two keepers standing around the cage, which was dimly lit by a small light bulb that cast an eerie glow. Chelsea was lying on her side, her bulging sides heaving as she panted.

"How's she doing?" Aaron asked.

"Not too good," Doc Rockwell said. "She's been in labor for the past hour, but nothing is happening. She's getting exhausted. I think something's terribly wrong."

Chapter Twelve

Aaron stared at the veterinarian in horror. "She's not going to die, is she?" he whispered. "Can't you do something, Doc?"

"I'm going to try," Doc Rockwell said. "We need to get her over to the infirmary immediately and find out exactly what the problem is." He glanced up from the struggling tigress and heaved a sigh of relief. "Good—here comes Walt with the tranquilizer gun! As soon as we get Chelsea sedated, we'll take her to the infirmary so I can check her out."

"But won't the sedation hurt the cubs?" Aaron asked anxiously.

Darlcnc kncw how much he loved Chelsea

and how eagerly he'd been looking forward to the birth of the cubs. Despite her anger with him and her hurt over what he'd done, her heart ached for Aaron. She reached out and grabbed his hand as they waited for Doc Rockwell to answer his question.

"Yes, it's possible," the veterinarian said. "But if we don't do this we're not only going to lose the cubs, we're going to lose Chelsea."

Aaron swallowed hard and squeezed Darlene's hand tightly. Together, Darlene and Aaron watched the cat keeper shoot a tranquilizing dart into Chelsea's flank.

"She barely moved when the dart hit her. She usually fights them." Aaron's voice was bleak and Darlene moved closer to him, wishing there were something she could do or something she could say to make him feel better.

The men gently lifted the tigress's limp body onto a wheeled table and pushed it into the infirmary. Aaron and Darlene tried to follow them into the operating room, but Doc Rockwell shook his head.

"Sorry, kids," Doc Rockwell said. "You'll have to wait out here. I'll let you know what's happening as soon as I know myself." He closed the door behind him.

"I can't believe this is happening!" Aaron said, pacing back and forth in front of the bench where Darlene was sitting.

"Aaron, why don't you sit down?" Darlene suggested. "You aren't going to help Chelsea by wearing a hole in the floor."

He slumped into the chair next to hers and looked at her, a strange expression on his face. "You want to hear the craziest part of all? I'm beginning to think you were right all along."

"Right about what?" Darlene asked, puzzled.

"About zoos." He heaved a deep sigh. "If Chelsea had been in a jungle tonight, she'd have been a goner for sure. At least with Doc Rockwell right there she has a fighting chance."

"It's funny, but just the other day I was thinking that maybe *you* were right all along," Darlene admitted.

"What do you mean?"

"We got a baby kangaroo in the nursery the other day while you weren't there. Doc had to perform emergency surgery on his foot because he got it caught in a broken piece of fencing. That's when I started thinking maybe you were right. Maybe animals shouldn't be kept in captivity."

Aaron smiled faintly. "Weird, isn't it? It took something like this for us to see each other's point of view."

"I'm not saying that I've suddenly become against zoos," Darlene warned him. "I still think it's important for there to be places where people can see animals and learn about them."

He nodded.

"But there's got to be a happy medium," she continued, "something between this kind of zoo with all the cages and returning the animals to their natural habitats."

"There is. That's what the animal rights group I told you about is looking into now," Aaron told her. "They've decided not to try to close the Glendale Zoo, but they're going to insist on some major changes."

"Like what?" Darlene asked, glad he had found something to take his mind off Chelsea, at least for the moment.

"They've hired an architect who's working

on a set of plans to house and display the animals in more natural environments. No more cages," Aaron explained. "Bears and lions and tigers can't jump very far, so they could be kept in open areas with wide moats around them. There are lots of ways to keep animals under control without locking them up in cages."

They both jumped as the door to the operating room flew open and Doc Rockwell came out.

"How's Chelsea?" Aaron asked anxiously, once again grabbing for Darlene's hand as if he needed her for support.

Doc Rockwell gave them both a huge grin. "Chelsea is fine, and so are all four of her cubs!"

"*Four?*" Darlene repeated, amazed. "No wonder she was having a hard time!"

Aaron whooped with joy and grabbed Darlene, hugging her so tightly he took her breath away. She giggled, giddy with excitement and relief.

"Would you two like to come in and see Glendale Zoo's newest arrivals?" Doc asked, still grinning. They followed him into the operating room. Chelsea was still asleep on the table, but on the floor in a basket were four perfect little tiger cubs.

"They're adorable," Darlene whispered.

"The problem was the biggest one," Doc Rockwell said. "Apparently he decided he wasn't sure he wanted to be born. He got all twisted up and I had to give him a helping hand."

Aaron gazed down at the cubs in silence, and Darlene knew he was feeling exactly the same sort of awe she felt. She was suddenly overwhelmed with sadness. Why had things turned out for her and Aaron the way they had? She cared about him more than she'd ever cared about a guy before, but even though they were close to agreeing on the zoo issue, how could she forget that he had tried to get her fired?

"Are you sure she's all right?" Aaron asked Doc Rockwell, petting Chelsea's sleek side.

The vet nodded. "She's fine. She'll probably sleep for quite a while, though."

"Aaron, now that all the excitement is over, would you mind taking me home?" Darlene hated to ask him, but it was getting late and she didn't want to make her parents come and get her.

"Sure." Aaron gave Chelsea one final pat. Then he and Darlene left the infirmary and went out into the night. "It's really something, isn't it?" he said, his voice still holding a touch of wonder as they got into his car. "No matter whether it's tiger cubs being born, or puppies, or kittens, it never fails to amaze me. Giving birth has got to be the biggest miracle in the world!"

Darlene nodded silently and got into the car. Neither of them spoke as Aaron drove her home. When he pulled up in front of her house, he parked the car, took off his seat belt, and faced her. "I'm glad you were able to come with me tonight," he said.

"Me, too," she murmured. Why couldn't she hate him?

"Darlene, I know you said that you didn't want to go out with me again, but I was wondering if maybe you might change your mind." In the light from the dashboard his eyes were warm and pleading as he gazed at her. "I just feel like we're so right for each other, and I kind of thought you felt that way, too."

Tears sprang to Darlene's eyes. "Yes, I *did* think we were right for each other—until the day you tried to get me fired," she said bitterly.

Aaron stared at her in what appeared to be genuine astonishment. "What are you talking about?"

"Oh, Aaron, don't pretend you don't know!" Darlene glared at him. "It was the Monday after our date. I went to find you, to talk to you about what had happened between us. That's when I overheard you talking to Ben Walkman, telling him I didn't care about the animals and I shouldn't be working in the nursery."

"I wasn't talking about you, I was talking about Ellen!" Aaron exclaimed.

Darlene's eyes widened. "Ellen?"

"Yeah—Ellen spends more time following her boyfriend around the zoo than she does taking care of the animals in the nursery. Ben asked me how I thought she was doing, and I had to tell him the truth." He looked at Darlene, shaking his head. "You honestly thought I was talking about *you*? You thought I wanted you to lose your job?"

Darlene was unable to speak for a moment and joy filled her heart. She nodded, a happy glow spreading through her. "I thought you were getting back at me for not agreeing with you about zoos."

"Now that we have that straightened out, are you willing to go out with me again?"

Darlene felt her toes curling in her sneakers, a sure sign that things were looking better between them. But she said, "I'm not sure. There's one more thing we need to get straightened out. All the girls warned me that you're a one- or two-date kind of guy. If I go out with you again, is it going to be our last date? Because if it is, I don't want to go. I couldn't stand going through a week like this past one ever again." She flushed slightly at her own boldness in asking him this question, but she had to know.

Aaron smiled ruefully. "Yeah, I guess they would say that. Last summer, I dated everyone. I'd see somebody new and think, maybe she's the girl for me. And then I'd take her out, but it never worked. Something was always missing. So this summer, I decided I was going to take it real slow, get to really *know* a girl before I finally asked her out. That's why it took me so long to ask you for a date. I wanted to be sure you were the right one."

"And am I?" Darlene whispered.

He grinned at her. "Let's just say that Chelsea has now become my *second* favorite girl. You're my first." And with those words he leaned over and gave Darlene a kiss that left no doubt in her mind whatsoever.